THE UNCIVIL WAR OF ANTHONY SEDLEY

The Personal Cost of War

Pauline Gregg

Edited and revised by Ros Meiggs

ISBN-13: 9798545612819

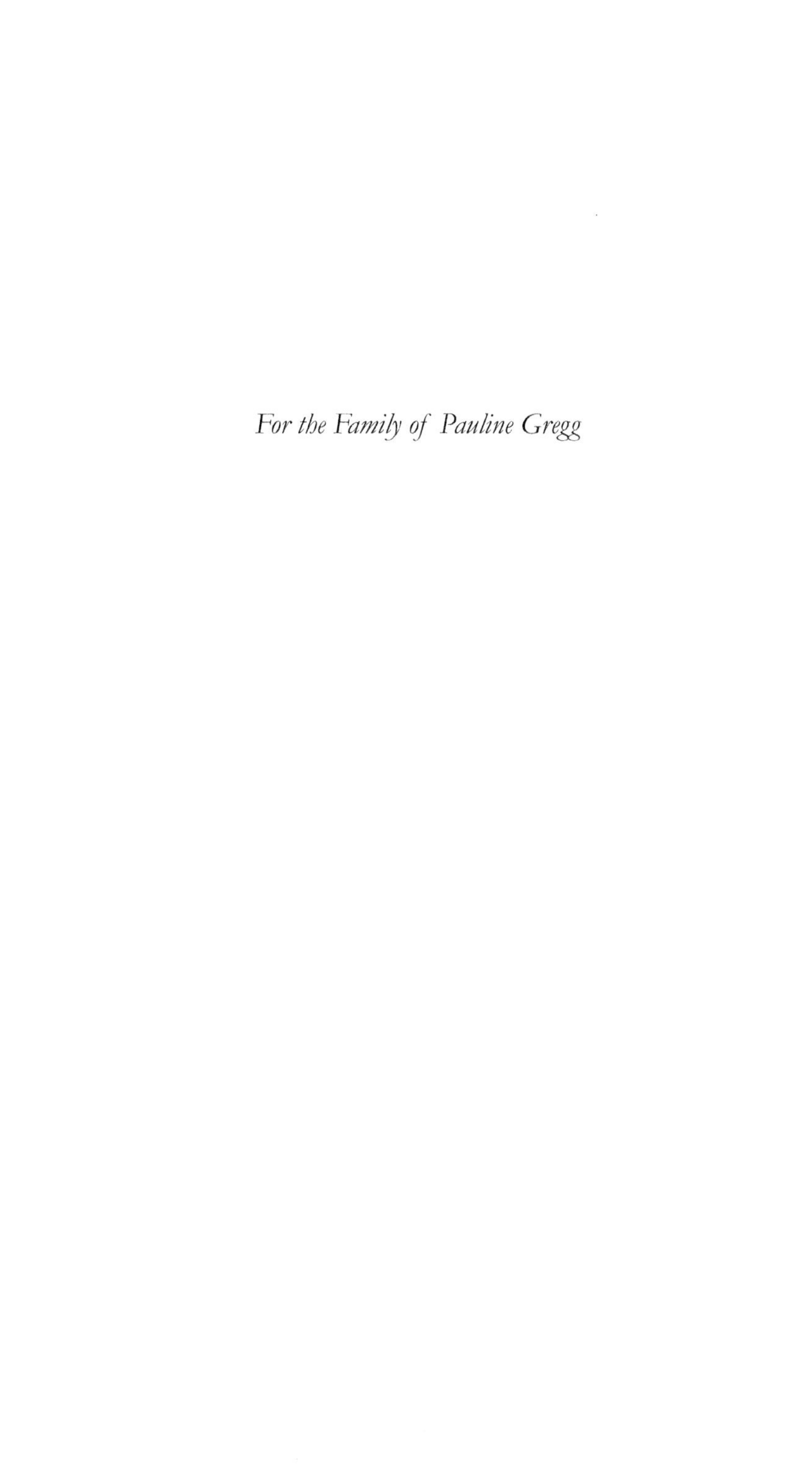

For the Family of Pauline Gregg

Many thanks to my husband Alan Barwise for his encouragement, to my daughter Ellie for all her interest and patient technical support, to my sister and brother-in-law Sylvia and Barry Williamson for their enthusiasm and help with this project. A sincere thank you to Janey Petterson who so willingly took the Burford photographs and shared them.

ABOUT THE AUTHOR

Pauline Gregg (1909–2006) was one of the first generations of women who seized the opportunity to combine higher education, political activism and a distinguished career with family life. She won a place at the London School of Economics and later wrote 'It was as if someone had opened the door to an enchanted life. My socialism had a focus, a new meaning.' She married Russell Meiggs, a classics fellow at Balliol College, Oxford. She found housework dull and instead would cycle every day to the Bodleian

Library where she continued her research on the seventeenth century. Her doctorate on the Leveller leader, John Lilburne, became the biography *Free-Born John*. *A Social and Economic History of Britain* became a standard reference work. She also wrote biographies of Charles I and Oliver Cromwell. C.V. Wedgwood described the former as 'the fullest and most carefully compiled that we are ever likely to see.' Her last years were spent writing a novel, the story of Anthony Sedley. I am aware of how much research she did into original pamphlets, letters and news-sheets which have survived from that articulate age to reveal a sensitive man who is deeply troubled by the horror of war. It has been my great joy and challenge, as her younger daughter, to bring this story to print.

CONTENTS

PREFACE

I grew up with the clickety click sound of my mother's Underwood typewriter. Pauline Gregg was a historian who wrote about social and economic history and about the troubled 17th century, publishing biographies of John Lilburne, Charles I and Oliver Cromwell. She often took her children and, in later years, her grandchildren, to Burford Church to tell the story of Anthony Sedley. He was one of 340 soldiers who, protesting against arrears of pay and the order to be prepared to go to Ireland, was rounded up by Cromwell and imprisoned in the church under sentence of death. It was here that he carved his name on the lead round the font.

At the age of 76 in 1985 my mother started to write a novel about Anthony Sedley, of whom there are no further historical facts. She continued to write and revise well into her eighties, leaving her family six different versions, some incomplete and all with pages missing. The task of making a complete story out of all the versions always seemed overwhelming until the prospect of an extended lockdown loomed. What better time to spread out the pages on the kitchen floor and at the same age as she was when she started writing. Some versions are in the third person but I believe telling the story in the first person, as in her later versions, makes it more compelling. I have edited, adapted and rewritten part of the story but it is still very much my mother's story of Anthony Sedley. You won't find any analysis of battles fought but you will find the background story to those battles and the story of a man deeply troubled by 'the Hell of War'.

Ros Meiggs
June 2021

INTRODUCTION

The Civil War of the seventeenth century stands out as a momentous episode in English history. It is a story that has many interpretations. There was relative peace and economic prosperity until Charles 1 dissolved Parliament. The public were incensed, opposing both the introduction of taxes without the authority of Parliament and ecclesiastic reforms. The social and political upheaval that followed turned lives upside down and left many, like Anthony Sedley, confused about what they were fighting for when faced by the horrors of war.

1

HARVESTING

I would like to start in the dim church at the end of my story, waiting for death. But an end supposes a beginning. Without it you will not know me. If I can tell my story with truth and understanding you may, with God's help, be able to judge me fairly. But my thoughts are random, my recollections run on, not always in sequence. The pictures come and go...

Looking back on those years as the man I now am, I will try to see the past as it was and not alter that past.

First and always in my memory is the big house near Banbury where I was born in the year 1625, the year King Charles came to the throne. Even now I can picture the house with its barns and dairy, the gardens enclosed by a brick wall taller than my father, the dining room where the tables were spread with all manner of meats and tarts, the long gallery with oak panels, the winter and summer parlours, the bedrooms with tapestry hung walls and beds enclosed by heavy curtains. I can smell the sweet smell of baking and roasting and forget the swarms of black flies that hovered near the food. I see the kitchen strewn with roses, such a picking, plucking and shredding of roses was there to make the Honey of Roses.

It was here that my father, John, conducted his business of merchant and clothier. The bales of cloth were brought in from the weavers' cottages and were stacked in the big barn until the carriers were ready to take them to London. I believed that we were well-off and I knew that my father was held in good respect in Banbury. But I also heard my father say:

'My eldest son must marry a Vivers or a Fletcher. We need to draw the businesses together. There's not enough trade for us all. We fall over each other and keep prices down.'

My father spoke like a judge, 'balanced' the neighbours called him. When he talked, I was not quite sure which side of the argument he was on. But with my brother Robert there was no doubt. He was slow of speech, emphatic in his beliefs, following all the preachers in Banbury and coming home full of the antics of the 'Roaring Boy'. He would hear no good of the King and spoke of Buckingham as an 'evil influence':

'All you can say in the King's favour,' he once proclaimed, 'is that he's better since Felton's knife finished Buckingham.'

I can remember I was shocked to hear that the killing of any man could be referred to as a good thing.

But that was my fault. I was too gentle, perhaps too dispassionate, to take sides easily. I was not stirred to the righteous wrath with which a good Christian or a good citizen should meet the iniquities of Church or State.

In all things physical Robert excelled, whether it was running, wrestling or playing football with the other boys. He managed the heavy tasks of the Sedley business with the greatest of ease. How or why he became so devoutly Puritan we never knew. Perhaps his friendship with the Fiennes of Broughton Castle had something to do with it, for nowhere in the country were there more devout Puritans.

'No place up at Broughton unless you're prepared for chapel every day and twice on Sunday,' my mother would say.

Robert was the idol of the neighbourhood with his ready smile, his mane of curly hair, his broad shoulders and his willingness to help anyone. When we talked of the worsening situation between the King and his subjects Robert would bang his great fist on the table and declare that the sooner they fought for their views the better. But my father would shake his head and speak of impetuosity while my mother quietly removed the dishes.

I, for my part, would sometimes try to talk to Robert of other things that were increasingly on my mind. It was shortly before the war started that I ventured to speak of my love of images and pictures.

'Can't you say,' I asked, 'it is indeed a beautiful object and love it as such? Must you be accused of idolatry because you admire a statue of the Virgin? Is it idolatry to see beauty in a representation of the Virgin, of Mary Magdalen, of Jesus himself? Is it only idolatry when the picture, the statue, is set up in Church? If you admire a Raphael Madonna in a gallery or in someone's house are you still guilty of idol worship? Is it the place as much as the object that counts?'

As Robert remained silent, collecting his thoughts, I put before him the book of paintings I had recently acquired.

'Or is it only the subject that matters?' I persisted. 'Is it idolatrous to admire a Venus of Giorgione or the magnificent Titian? May you look upon a Botticelli Venus rising from the foam… ?'

It was not long before Robert's fist rose in the air.

'That's lust!' he exclaimed harshly, 'that's carnal sin.'

'Idolatry, lust, carnal sin,' I pondered, 'how do I recognise them? Has beauty no place in the Puritan worship?'

'Beauty!' cried Robert, 'there's beauty in the fields, in the sheep with their lambs; there's beauty in the creamy fleece that the spinners turn into yarn, beauty in the yarn the weavers make into cloth, and in the great bales of cloth stored here in our father's barn. I tell ye Anthony, there's so much beauty in all the things around you that you have no need of graven images. How can paint and canvas or stone or bronze compare with what the Lord has given us? I see beauty all around me as I go about my work. When I commune with God, I have no need for more. I thrust all else aside. It's only me and the Lord, nothing to come between us, neither graven image nor coloured pictures.'

'What about the "Roaring Boy"?' I ventured, amazed at my brother's vehemence, at his unaccustomed fluency of speech.

'I shut him out,' said Robert simply, 'whether he's there or not, it makes no difference. It's only me and the Lord. The 'Roaring Boy' is only good for unbelievers, for those of little faith.'

How I longed for such simplicity of belief! But how right he was in the beauty of the fields and the animals and our own gentle, quiet countryside. Yet man can create beauty too, I pondered, with his hands, with the help of his eyes, with the working of his spirit. Need there be a rift between them? Perhaps it was only the poet who knew the answer. Thus, my determination to be a writer, a poet, took shape.

Hannah was a year younger than Robert and three years my senior. People thought she was pretty with her fair hair and blue eyes and it was no wonder that one of the Fiennes boys had taken up with her. John lived at Broughton Castle, the third son of Lord Saye and Sele. We knew a Sedley would not be considered a fitting match, '… a lord's a lord and a tradesman's a tradesman,' but I think I presumed too much upon a man who had the good of all upon him, and who suffered for it too.

Visits with John to the moated castle where he lived were high spots of school holidays. I badly wanted to find out more about the secret passage, its entrance some quarter of a mile from the castle, whose whereabouts was known only to a few. But outside, where the passage ended amid tangled briars and overgrown bushes, Hannah and John would meet while some of us kept guard, not unduly interested in what was going on. As I grew older, I became indignant that my sister should not be considered good enough for a Fiennes. But I also thought she'd be happier if she married someone like the Fletcher boy who, they said, was making himself ill over her. Robert and Hannah, being close in age, were much together.

Also part of my life for as long as I can remember were the Eliots and the Eliot farm. Uncle Fred was my mother's brother. Aunt Margery was Fred's wife who had brought with her a little girl from her first marriage whom I always considered Rose Eliot, a sweet and beautiful name. Everyone talked of her as my half-cousin, perhaps to make it clear there was no blood shared between us. There was always talk that we would marry, it was my thought too, though what was Rose's view I never considered and she never considered it either.

I remember her so clearly as she was then. In particular the way she had of seeming to hug herself when she was pleased, a drawing together of arms and shoulders with a little smile that brought dimples round her mouth. And how, when tired, she would press her cheekbones with her finger tips on each side of her face.

'Tired, Rose?' I would ask after a long day gathering truant sheep from the far fields. Then we would go inside and collect milk and Margery's little honey cakes from the big farm kitchen and take them to our secret hideaway.

Old Ben, Rose's grandfather, her mother's father, lived with them too. He was always 'Old Ben' to us, though he had energy enough in the day and was a good talker. Only in the evening, summer and winter alike, whether or not a fire was burning in the hearth or the sun was shining outside, he would retire to his chimney corner with his long clay pipe and puff contentedly in silence. He could not be disturbed then, but at other times he would tell us stories of the wars he had taken part in, of the siege of Breda, of Mansfeldt's ill-fated army, of sailing to intercept Spanish treasure ships, of the magnificent futility of Buckingham.

'No man could tell how many died,' he once

sighed, 'take Cadiz and the Isle of Rhe together. On the voyage home from Spain, they tipped the bodies overboard like unwanted ballast and I escaped with naught but this!' And he thrust forward his left hand with the three missing fingers. 'But it's summat a man don't forget…'

I would gaze in awe at the gnarled and misshapen hand and wonder at the nature of old Ben's thoughts as he sat there in the chimney corner at night. And I wondered at the lines and creases on his face, the skin browned from long campaigns. And to those lines of age were added those of laughter, care and contemplation, all etched deeply to a darker hue. I have seen apples, long forgotten, of such a wrinkled sight, or dried out walnuts the colour of Old Ben's face.

Rose's little half-brothers, the children of Fred and Margery, were twins, and to the market in Banbury we would all go many a time. We would stuff ourselves with Banbury cakes and sing songs round the Cross, though it was not the old Cross, we learnt, as that was Popish and had been torn down by the Puritans years before.

A special time we were there was in May 1630 to celebrate the birth of a son to King Charles and his French Queen. Why, I must have been a mere five years old. All the world had come to market to eat roast pork and sweet cakes: Sedleys, Eliots, Vivers, Barbers, Lockiers, Hawtens from Galthorpe and many more of my father's merchant friends. Guns were fired from Banbury Castle and there were fireworks in the market place. I remember how Rose and I squealed with delight to find the side shows: a juggler with five knives, a lady in a glittering dress dancing on a tightrope, the puppets who danced around and sang in strange voices. We sat under the trestle tables which were laden with soft Banbury cheeses, spicy Banbury cakes, the buns so full of currants you could hardly see the dough, eating our fill. The Banbury ale was not for us but quantities enough were drunk.

Conversations fluttered on the breeze: Aunt Margery and my mother pleased that the Queen had a baby at last; a man laughing, 'a baby's done more for the King's image than aught else; you'd think he'd achieved summat special, summat for US!' And then, loud and clear, was William Whately, the Puritan minister:

'No good will come of this heathen rejoicing for a Popish brat,' he was saying and his voice rose loudly over the crackle of the fireworks and the bursting of the rockets, even indeed over the firing of the guns. I had always felt pride in the 'Roaring Boy' of Banbury, such was he known as, but I recall how even then my anger rose as the great voice cut into our merrymaking.

'Shame on ye! Shame on ye for rejoicing at a Papist's spawn! Rather repent for the coming among us of the Horn of the Beast that will surely smite us like the Bull of Bashan and drive us into hell fire unless we repent and turn out the whole brood of corruption…'

This is how his words come back to me as I write, this is how I learned the Puritan teaching.

The Eliot children stayed in our big house that night, Hannah and Rose together in a bed, I and my brother in another and the Eliot twins laughing and giggling in a third. I remember my father saying that evening, 'Aye but there's plague in London. Why rejoice?'

Aunt Margery adding, 'No good omen for a birth.'

My mother, as was her custom, added a cheerful note:

'Bless my soul, there's always plague somewhere! There was plague over at Aston when our Hannah was born. But don't think I didn't rejoice.'

When I was older there was another market day in Banbury when Rose rode in from the farm on an old white farm horse and caused much laughter as they all chanted:

'Ride a cock-horse
To Banbury Cross
To see a fine lady
Upon a white horse.'

She had let her hair down that day and without the kerchief she usually wore the thick brown hair, tangled from her ride, fell below her shoulders. Our mood was dashed when the Puritan minister stormed out of the chapel.

'Cover up!' he cried. 'Get you gone for a wanton! Where's your kerchief, girl?' His eyes went to Rose's legs in their fine blue stockings, her skirts tucked up to make riding easier. We all followed his gaze. The minister, I swear, looked longer than he need have done. The Puritan fathers looked stern, many of the women were shocked, or pretended to be, I know not. I knew nothing but a blinding rage as I saw the colour mount in Rose's face, the tears spring to her eyes.

'Get thee gone for a wanton!' shouted the preacher again.

'Nay,' I shouted back. 'She's Rose Eliot come to market and she works on her father's farm all the week and comes to service on Sunday. She's a good girl!' and I made to seize the horse's bridle and lead her away. But the city fathers were at one with the minister, though they spoke more kindly.

'She's a child still,' one of them said. At that moment my mother came, pushing through the little crowd. I could see that she too was angry. 'Keep your tongue and your hellfire for those that deserve it,' she cried. 'Rose Eliot and her family are as good Puritans as any in this parish!'

She helped Rose to dismount and marshalled all the children into Meg's parlour where we were served with cakes and sharp apple juice. I remember that my mother made no attempt to cover Rose's hair, though her skirts were now down over her knees.

We stayed late that evening in Banbury. It was my mother's way, I knew, of making up to us for the minister's conduct. The older boys played football in the streets and as the autumn evening drew to a close the alehouses showed their long poles with bushes atop to show their readiness to serve ale. Uncle Fred and Old Ben were in the Unicorn with my father and other men talking serious business. When my mother hustled the children away, we all piled, happy and sleepy into the big cart to make our way home. Rose and I, as so often, sat close together. Her hair was still loose and smelled of hay and lavender.

That was a day I have never forgotten. In all my later allegiance to the Puritan cause there was always a reluctance, a questioning, a harking back to a religion of greater beauty, a less unhappy and more joyous worship. As a child I was, indeed, frightened by many of the Puritan preachers. When my father would say, 'It's the "Roaring Boy" today' and marshal us all to the chapel or market place I would hang back, seeking some excuse to stay behind. I developed a resentment that 'a Banbury man' came to imply a Puritan. I think of the verse:

'To Banbury came I, O prophane one!
Where I saw a Puritan one
Hanging of his cat on Monday
For killing of a mouse on Sunday.'

The very lines I was punished for whispering to young Vivers at school! John Vivers who, they say, ran away at Edgehill but who fought so fiercely at Brentford for he was imprisoned with Lilburne in Oxford Castle. And little Tom Hawtry, who took up the verse and passed it on to his neighbour in class. He was punished too, invalided out of the army and married his childhood sweetheart. They had an idiot child. How quickly life moves! There we were, at school together tittering in class, the worst that could happen the schoolmaster's cane. And now John

Vivers forever with the ignominy of cowardice, and Tom Hawtry with an idiot child. How little marks the child from the man, yet how much.

How little, indeed, lies between birth and death. There was my brother Jamie, born and died in a day. And then in quick years Charles and Mary, but they lived no more than a week. We followed the little coffins to the grave and my mother said the Lord did not intend her to have more children. But then in 1638 came Nick, who flourished from his beginning and grew into a cheerful boy with all the good looks and all the charm of Robert and Hannah. He was my mother's greatest comfort during the war years. In those last carefree days before the outbreak of war he would follow us on his chubby legs down to the Cherwell, plunging through the banks of the river and learning to swim in the eddying river. I can hear his shrieks of glee when he set our little boat rocking as we set off for a day's picnic. How easy, even now, to be back in Cherwell country.

2

The River Cherwell as it flows south from Banbury to Oxford winds with many a twist and turn through some of the gentlest, greenest country in the world until it joins the Thames at Oxford. With its trees, its meadows, its sweetness, it is a river easy to have pleasure with, like the gentle undulating country on its banks. In the Cherwell valley or lands adjacent many prosperous families had made their homes. The great houses were small compared with those in other parts of the country, but this was fitting and accorded well with the nature of the land: the Fiennes family at Broughton, the Verneys at Claydon, Sir Robert Dormer at Rousham. Walter Jones had built a fine house at Chastleton at the beginning of the century. He was a Witney wool merchant with whom grandfather Sedley had had close dealings. The continued friendship between the two families brought us on more than one occasion to romp in the long gallery at Chastleton which was so long that we ran races there and bowled our hoops from end to end.

It is this Cherwell that flashes through my mind whenever I think about those days. We would ride or walk for miles over the surrounding countryside. We knew where to find the biggest blackberries, the bright yellow crab-apples, the little orange japonica. Mushrooms we would fetch on any dewy September morning, bringing home only the freshest and the best. We would seek out the enormous bright yellow kingcups that were the pride of the valley, or the strange snake's head fritillaries that frightened Rose with a portent of evil but fascinated me with their strange beauty.

Sometimes we came upon evidence of ancient peoples who had walked the Cherwell valley long before.

'Think,' I would say to Rose as we came upon the ancient British camp at Arberry Hill, 'how our ancestors fought to defend themselves! The Romans too must have been marching through our countryside. They settled too. They found the farming good. But it must have been hard on the ancient Britons,' I added as we sat on the highest tier of what must have been a Roman amphitheatre in Berrymoor field outside Banbury.

Once we made an expedition to the Rollright Stones with my father who pointed out the importance of their position on the top of the range of hills which marked the boundary between the tableland of Oxfordshire and the great Vale of Warwickshire. We paced the great circle, some 107 feet round (I still remember), gazed up at the King's stone nearly nine feet high and the group my father called the Five Whispering Knights. We wondered at the meaning of it all. Some pagan worship perhaps? We could only wonder and Rose, as she was wont to do, shivered with fear of the unknown.

Rose was happier by far on Barrow Hill, the tumulus we would climb on a fine, clear day to get the view of nine counties from the top. 'You see, Rose', I would say, 'Why they say that we live in the heart of England'. Rose would smile and nestle close to me as I kissed her with the clumsiness of young love. I did not want to take Rose for granted, so one day I gave her the most beautiful rose I could find in the walled garden and carefully copied out Edmund Waller's verse:

'Go lovely Rose
Tell her that wastes her time and me,
That now she knows,
When I resemble her to thee
How sweet and fair she seems to be.'

We loved the corn mill on the Sar Brook. I

remember the red, rich soil of that good corn-growing land and the colour of the landscape – red, then speckled green, then entirely green, and finally golden with the ripened corn. We would go to the mill after harvest when the miller, not much older than I was, would welcome us and take us into his well-supplied house by the mill for refreshment. There were fulling mills too, and a paper mill, but we liked the smell of the corn mill best. The woad mill at Broughton, near the castle, was exciting for us with the deep blue dye which gave colour to the weavers' cloth. We would steal a bit to paint ourselves like the ancient Britons and maybe I would smuggle a bit into the schoolroom.

Our play would take us sometimes up to Runyon's farm, a remote farmstead in a little hollow whose owners kept to themselves more than other families. They said George Runyon chose seclusion after his wife's death and had lived there alone with his mother and a little girl. It was a place apart in its isolation, while a feeling of tragedy that hung over the farm made it for us a place of mystery, even awe. We would crawl through the surrounding undergrowth on our bellies to get a view of the farm buildings.

'Two carts, four horses, three farmhands in view,' I would whisper and Rose would take note of my findings. Such a crackling of twigs and rustling of bracken was there that the dog would start barking and a voice would call out:

'It's the Sedley children again!'

Sometimes we would dare each other to go to the door and ask for a drink of water. We finally did on the day when an irresistible smell of baking wafted up from the farmhouse kitchen. We were hungry and we ventured down.

'We can't ask for food,' Rose whispered, 'only a drink of water.'

As we slowly approached the farmhouse door the old lady came to the door and she was smiling, rewarding us with a mug of cool, sweet milk and slices of steaming bread straight from the oven.

'I wondered when you'd venture down,' she said.

After that the farm lost some of its mystery and we would often stop for a drink, accompanied as often as not by a pie or a tart which seemed to be always fresh from the oven. We would sometimes be intrigued by the sight of a wispy, long-haired girl, untidily dressed, who would dart in from the cow byre or the stable or the pen where the sheep were lambing, eye us all for a moment or two then dart away again.

'Nan,' her grandmother would call, 'come and talk

with the children.'

'Come and play!' we would chorus. But Nan was gone.

'She's used to her wild ways,' the old lady said, 'ever since her mother died. Prefers animals to us,' she added sadly. 'She has her own way with them, and with us. Wilful she is as well as wild.'

Sometimes we crossed the common to the tangled heath beyond the weavers' cottages where old Sarah Trollope had lived alone for ever, or so it seemed. People said she lived in a 'hovel', that her house was 'tumbledown'. But when Rose and I ventured near it collecting blackberries it looked very neat. Rose said there were curtains at the windows which was more than we had, except in the big drawing room where my mother entertained her guests with cards and music. But as children we had believed that old Sarah was a witch. Why, they said, she had cured young Davey Newsome of a cough that had lasted for over a year and that Farmer Nixon's cows, who had passed too close to her cottage, all died within a week of each other. Another time she took a stranger boy into her house and mended his broken leg. He had been found down by the river and no-one knew how he got there. Some said he had stolen a horse that threw him and bolted. But the horse was never found and there had been no hue and cry for a missing horse, a missing boy neither. So old Sarah mended his leg and took him to live with her, naming him Will. It was the will of God, she said, that he should have fallen so near her cottage, for no-one else could have restored that twisted limb. She considered some time about a second name. To name him Trollope seemed hardly right. Yet she wanted him to have a second name so she called him Cherwell, after the river where he was found. Will Cherwell went to the village school and grew up strong and well, before whom no-one dared cast remarks about old Sarah.

When things were going well in the weavers' village, when harvests were good, the cows calved without trouble and the lambs skipped merrily in the fields; when maids went courting and children played happily, when there was food for all and mothers gave birth easily to healthy babies, little notice was taken of Sarah Trollope. She was called, half affectionately, 'old Sarah' or 'Ma Trollope'. Mothers would sometimes come for a potion to cure a child's cough that kept them awake at night. After Sarah's success with Will Churchill's leg men, who had injured themselves in the fields or caught their fingers in the loom, would come to her to be healed. Maids looking for husbands would creep down to old Sarah after dark, while wives longing for children would seek her out.

It was when harvests were bad, when winter gales tore at the elm trees and snatched the roofs off their cottages, when streams overflowed flooding the meadows and drowning the sheep, when murrain struck the cattle, when children fell ill and babies died before they were born that old Sarah became a witch. There was talk of her black cat with green eyes and the toad which a child had seen squatting by her door. And people remembered that she bore the marks of a witch: a large mole on her cheek from which grew seven hairs. Seven was the witch number. It was said at such times of dearth and sickness that inside her cottage were the phials and lotions she used for her spells, together with the dismembered newts and spiders, frogs and lizards that were the materials of her trade.

Children who peered through the windows of her cottage swore they had seen waxen images stuck with pins. A child once woke screaming in the night crying that Sarah was coming to take him away. Tongues spared no spite to claim that Sarah was trying to make the boy sign a compact with the devil and that only purity of spirit had saved him.

When shortly afterwards a weaver's wife died in childbirth and two children died of smallpox, when a mare died and the dog that ate the carcass died also there was no holding back of the villagers. An angry crowd tied old Sarah by her thumbs and great toes and made a large untidy bundle of her. She was to be thrown into the village pond. If she floated, she was certainly a witch, otherwise she would simply drown but would be free of the stigma of witchcraft. That was when my father rode among his workers, lashing out with his whip and commanding the old lady be untied. He held a court of law there and then.

'If there is any evidence of witchcraft,' he said, 'Sarah Trollope goes to the Assizes with good witnesses to prove the case against her. If there is no evidence, back you go to your homes, and Sarah to hers. But one thing I will not tolerate among those who work for me is self-imposed trial and punishment.'

I had never before or since seen my father show such vehemence, sternness and authority. They had their effect and the weavers sullenly untied Sarah. She came to my father, gaining her feet clumsily and with difficulty. Someone laughed as she stumbled. I felt proud of my father as he stepped forward, raised the old lady to a standing position and offered her his arm. As she took it, raising herself to her full stature, she thanked him courteously. I noted that her voice was gentle and controlled and she spoke more like my father in accent and inflection than like the weavers. It seemed, indeed, as though she were no stranger to taking a gentleman's arm.

That evening my father reminded us that forty or fifty people had suffered death as witches in the reign of the present king's father. The ordeal of trial by water, from which Sarah Trollope had just been saved, was not uncommon.

'I fear for a nation that can entertain such superstition in its midst,' he said.

'But,' remarked my mother, 'it was King James himself who set the example. He believed in witches. Didn't he say it was witches who raised the seas against him when he brought his Queen home from Denmark?'

'And,' Robert added, 'didn't the present Queen herself consult a witch about her pregnancy?'

'Hush, boy, hush. That's something we don't talk about,' whispered my mother.

There was concern enough about Sarah Trollope for me to be sent up the following day to her cottage with a piece of game pie, a few delicacies from the Sedley larder and the hope that she was none the worse for her experience. I called for Rose on my way. To see inside Sarah's cottage was an excitement I must share with Rose. So together we approached the door where there was no toad, only the black cat frisking about. We lifted the latch and found Sarah sitting beside the fire, the room neat and warm. Will Cherwell came in shortly after, he had been out when the weavers came for his mother (for so he always called her) and I could see the anger flash as he cried out 'I'd have killed them that took her.' We shared milk and honey cakes and she showed us to a smaller room where, indeed, were rows of coloured bottles and little heaps of powder, chopped leaves and roots, a pile of newly picked plants, some open books and a pretty little silver scales.

'I can cure the cough in children and help the ague in their parents, fevers too,' she mused, holding one of her phials. 'And if they'd let me go among the sheep and cattle, I could help them too. You've never seen my cow, or one of my sheep fall down and die,' she said, fixing me with her bright blue eyes.

Indeed, I remember thinking that one of the charges brought against her was that she caused other animals to die while preserving her own.

'And now I'm trying to find a way with this cursed plague. The doctors do naught but bleed and leave their patients where they are. Put them in clean beds, wash out the vermin from the walls and cleanse their bodies with nature's own physic and you'd be nearer to a cure. Aye and nearer prevention too.'

She took up one of the phials which contained a reddish fluid and shook it angrily while she looked at her books.

As we left, I noticed the candles and the candlewax dripping down. How easy it would be for a child peering through the window to imagine that the dripping wax formed a human shape, like making pictures in the fire.

On our way home Rose's talk was only of how clean the cottage was. Scrubbed every day, she said.

3

The day the Players came to Broughton to perform the terrible tragedy of *Hamlet, Prince of Denmark*, was a day of big rejoicing. There was enough of suspense and fighting at the end of the play to keep the excitement going. Robert spoke of 'the inequity of words, the lewdness of men in women's clothes.' He did not come and this disappointed me, as he had disappointed me with 'graven images'.

For my part I wondered in awe at the dilemma of the young prince and wished that Ophelia and her father might have done more to help him. It was the words though that caught my imagination. I begged a copy of the play from my schoolmaster and learned by heart some of the big speeches, saying them over and over again not only for their meaning but for the sound of the words.

'Oh! That this too, too solid flesh would melt…' I would murmur as I went about some task in the home.

'Whether 'tis better in the mind to suffer…'

'What are you doing, muttering to yourself?' Hannah would ask, and I would try to get her ear to catch the magic of the sounds, even if her mind could not grasp the meaning of the words. But she only laughed, impatient to be off on some girl's task, maybe ironing her petticoat for her next meeting with the Fiennes boy.

The play made a deep impression on me as did the Player King for he came to speak to me after the performance. He had seemed an old man on the stage, but now he seemed quite young, tall and younger than my father.

'What are you called, boy?' he asked. 'Never have I seen a child so enthralled throughout a performance.' I found myself speaking to him of my love of words and how I would like to write a play like Will Shakespeare.

The following day I went up to Broughton to watch the Players' departure. They were folding costumes, packing them in tidy fashion in the carts that waited to take them to their next engagement. They brought out the big throne on which the King had been seated, there were boxes of beads and jewellery, the wigs which Ophelia and the Queen had worn, and the stage make-up with which they had painted their faces. It was strange to see the Players in their ordinary clothes and I tried to recognise Hamlet, Ophelia and the rest. The Player King came up with a hearty slap on the back.

'Farewell, Anthony Sedley! We'll meet again!' and so we did. But not for long years and in very different circumstances.

When I think of the Players I also think of the Gypsies. There was an area of heathland not far from old Sarah Trollope's cottage where they would arrive suddenly and unheralded and, so it seems in my memory, on a bright summer's day. They would stay for a week or two and then move off as silently and suddenly as they had come. I can still feel the delight when the cry went up 'The gypsies are here!' and the dismay when we would race out to the common after school to find it empty, bare of caravans, the camp fire extinguished, the noise and bustle silenced to the few hens and goats round Sarah's dwelling.

We loved the brightly coloured clothes the gypsies wore, especially their long cloaks spangled with stars and the crescent moon, their headdresses of beads and spangles that glittered in the sun and tinkled in the breeze. It was a wondrous sight when they danced to the beating of tambourines. Robert forbade us to join in the dance, but we took no heed and joined with the rhythmic beating of feet and clapping of hands. Hannah too, tossing her curls, joined in the wild traditional dances with the swarthy gypsy men like a bright jewel tossed from hand to hand.

We came to know Ezekiel, the leader of the gypsies, quite well. He was, it seemed, father or father-in-law or uncle or grandfather or even great-uncle or great-grandfather to all the rest who were, indeed, one large family. They showed us how to track an animal, to listen for the sounds a gamekeeper made from far away, to catch the scent of the wind, to interpret the rustling of a leaf.

The gypsies took no part in the quarrel between King and Parliament. Maybe they left their Midland haunts for areas far removed from the clash of battle. I often wondered why the sweet Midland counties bore so much of the brunt of war. Perhaps there was a stubbornness about these men of the soft centre of England, an independence of spirit fostered by the quiet interplay of family with family. They stood by what they came to believe. Would to God we had all made more sense of those tortured times.

And ever my mind goes back to Cherwell days. Up or down stream we knew every ripple in the water, every stone that caused an eddy, every little turn the stream made as it made its way to the Thames. We knew each hole in the river bank, where the mole had burrowed, where the water rat lived, where the little moorhen was protecting her brood. We heard the woodpecker, saw the kingfisher darting and flashing in the bright light. We had a little boat which we hid in the reeds and would push out through the sedgy river until we found enough water in mid-stream to float her, and then would let ourselves be carried down until the boat got wedged by the reeds. Once the boat capsized, flinging us amid shouts of laughter and fright into the cold water. We crept home, hoping to dry ourselves in the warm kitchen but the grown-ups were looking serious, discussing serious business round the big table. The words 'King' and 'Ship Money' were all that I could hear.

This really was, to me, the beginning. In the weeks that followed I heard more of such talk when many men would come to the house and gather round the big fireplace in the evening. No-one heeded me as I sat with my books or my carving in the far corner of the room. But the first time I was much involved was when I was sent with a message to my father in the Town Hall at Banbury. Many men were gathered there and someone was saying:

'Why talk of ships to us who are as far as could be from the sea?'

'Is that so?' asked old Bill Buzzard. He was always slow of thought and slow of speech. 'How far be we then from the sea?'

This continued while they all hazarded their guesses and gave their views about the ocean.

'Treacherous!' a voice called out loud and clear. 'Horses and wagons we can tend and mend. We can dig ourselves out of the mire in winter, but whoever dug himself out of the sea?'

There were titters at that, but my father was impatient to settle the issue.

'Anthony lad,' he called. 'Go along to school and find out from your books how far we are from the nearest sea.'

I sped away, knowing where to find the big atlas that Mr Thomas used. The school was open and I made my measurement, I could see we were surely in middle England.

'Speak up,' my father commanded on my return. And that was when I stood up and faced the men of Banbury. Whether I liked it or not for the first time I became part of a protest against the King.

'We're right in the middle,' I said. 'One hundred and fifteen miles to Harwich, or nearly.'

'And does a river flow from Banbury to the sea?' someone asked.

'No Sir.'

'Why then talk to us of ships? What good are ships to us?'

'There's Cherwell flows to Thames and Thames to sea,' I spoke up, amazed at my own boldness. But my father laughed. 'Cherwell will not take the ships the King is asking for. My friends, you draw, perhaps, the wrong conclusion. Keep our coasts free from enemy attack and you protect our inland shires as well.'

'Aye,' a voice spoke up, 'it's the country's defence we're asked to contribute to, and the sum's not large.'

'Defence!' cried another, 'what defences have any taxes given us but pirates round our shores, more clothes on the Queen's back and more pictures in the King's galleries!'

Next Fred Eliot, Rose's stepfather, was on his feet talking passionately 'Let us remember Buckingham and the Isle of Rhe. What happened to the money raised for that expedition? Did you ever see the sorry remnant of those men who returned? Or hear of those who never returned? But the King honoured Buckingham. And so it is now. Honour to the King's friends, the brunt to us. Ship money, my friends, large or small, is but taxation in another guise.'

It was all tangled up in my mind. Not money for ships but general defence. Not ships but money, but not ship money only taxation.

And now someone was talking more quietly. The

issue, he said, went beyond ship money to the general question of taxation. If they granted this, the second writ of ship money, it would become a regular tax and that they could not, would not, stand for. Why, it was an arbitrary tax, for the King ruling without Parliament had no authority to tax his people.

There were roars of approval at this and as we walked home together my father spoke to me for the first time of Lord Saye and Sele and John Hampden. It was likely, he said, that John Hampden would refuse to pay the ship money tax on his Stoke Mandeville estate and so bring the matter to Court for legal judgement.

'Old Subtlety planned it so,' he said, using for the first time in my hearing the name by which William Fiennes, first Viscount Saye and Sele, was known to his associates.

In the days that followed I thought much about the King. One summer day in 1635, not long after the ship money meeting, we were to go to Enstone where the King and Queen were visiting. We knew the King would want to see the waterworks and cascades of Thomas Bushell and indeed we did ourselves. Rose was puzzled as to what to wear and wanted to wear her very best for the Queen but her mother rebuked her saying her best would be no longer best after 15 miles or so of English roads. Indeed the Queen would not even look at her. This made Rose sad so I drew from under my coat the present I had for her. She opened it with cries of delight, holding the kerchief to her head. It matched the blue of her eyes perfectly. She wore it on that day as we stood on a little hillock and saw the King and Queen clearly as they left their coach and made for the cascades. I looked curiously at the man whom I had heard talked of as a tyrant because he had dismissed his Parliament six years before and had ruled without one ever since. But he didn't look like a tyrant, he just looked happy to be with his dainty little French wife. What surprised me most of all was his smallness and delicacy, the little steps he took as he made his way to the grotto. How different was that step from the farmers I knew who strode about the fields, or the merchants who walked with long, measured steps about Banbury. I saw Rose's delight and could see that she too thought they were not at all like tyrants.

'She doesn't look Popish,' Rose whispered, and I wondered what would be a Popish appearance.

Rose made her way through the crowd, gentle in all she did but purposeful. Soon we were at the very front with the men and ladies dressed in their very best who had ridden in their carriages to see the King and Queen. I saw the King's hair was free, dropping on his shoulders, his shirt open at the neck, breeches loosed at the knee. His doublet had slashes in the wide sleeves with embroidery round the cuffs like collars. His boots were of thick leather with square toe and big heel. Charles quickly saw us and smiled:

'We are h… h… h… happy that ch… children should c… c… c… come to see us.'

I had heard of the King's stammer but it was a shock to hear it. Then the Queen turned and patted Rose's head with the blue kerchief with a smile sweet and kind. We tried to bow and curtsy but felt awkward yet strangely elated. The awkwardness had gone by the time we reached home and the words spilled out as we told of our meeting with the King and Queen. Rose spoke long about the Queen's dress of green satin, cut low on her dainty shoulders and caught back to show a petticoat underneath, embroidered in soft colours. The full sleeves were open in front and brought together with a clasp which Rose swore was a diamond clasp. But there was a strange quietness in the room and our happiness was not shared.

'I wouldn't have a Papist touch my daughter,' growled Rose's father.

Robert bit his lip and said we should never have

gone, while Hannah only wanted to know more about what the Queen was wearing.

It was my father who spoke in measured tone, 'I believe he's a kind man. It was good of him to talk to a child with so many gentry around, How I wish he would free himself of evil counsellors.'

4

JOHN LILBURNE ON THE PILLORY

When Uncle Fred moved south to a small farmhouse and profitable land near Oxford, I missed the easy coming and going between the Sedley house and the Eliot farm.

'Sell out now,' Fred Eliot said, 'before the trouble starts. If land and farm is all you have, lose it and you lose all.'

And he went on to talk about the good market gardens around Oxford and to tell how he could rent land near the city and make a good profit from supplying the town and colleges.

'Good market gardens, good orchards, and if they're destroyed it's someone else's capital, not mine,' he concluded.

My father and Uncle Fred sat long discussing the rights and wrongs of the proposal and what good might come of it. But Fred had been thinking hard when he declared he would invest the proceeds of the sale of his land in the Providence Island Company that Lord Saye and Sele, Lord Brook and other good Puritans had established in the New World. There was much talk of setting up a God-fearing commonwealth that would forbid card-playing, whoring and drunkenness, but where in the world this was, I knew not.

Our visits to Oxford always ended with a visit to the Eliots and always started with my mother saying, 'Line your stomachs now, before we start'. But I preferred to wait for the strong, sweet smell of pies and bread at the Banbury coach stop. My father would drive us the short distance to Banbury, whipping up the horses so that the cart swayed as if to overturn in the deep ruts and my mother cried out for fear of spoiling her best market clothes. Hannah, in her prettiest cotton with her hair in ringlets would grip tightly. For Oxford was a place for boys, for young men, for scholars who were not all Puritans by any means. A dangerous place, my mother would say, for young girls, 'Better to hide yourself than show yourself.' But there was one indeed to whom Sue meant to show herself and I thought he'd likely be aware of her coming.

The day's pleasure started at the coach stop with a bite into the warm coffin and the taste of lamb with cloves, mace and nutmeg. It was followed by the pleasure of sitting on the Oxford coach, enjoying the pie and the passing landscape as we were jolted from side to side and flung against each other. 'Better on horseback! Even a post horse would be better than this!' my father would grumble.

In Oxford we would walk through the meadows to the majestic Thames and sometimes I would race along its banks to where our own Cherwell swelled its waters. I would look back to the city walls behind which college buildings rose in irregular forms and shapes and tell my father that I would go to Merton (I could see this most clearly) or St John's (it was the college I saw first as we entered the city from the north). My father laughed:

'A high ambition, boy! But Oxford smacks too much of something else that's 'high.' No High Church Chancellor shall clip your wings. It's Cambridge and Dr

Preston for you if you climb so high!'

Would I have climbed so high? Would I have become a student, read my books and maybe preached a sermon? But my thoughts must rest on the reality of the past rather than on broken surmises of what might have been…

It was down by the river while my mother dozed on a bench and my father strode away to complete his business that Hannah and young John Fiennes would meet. There were other young men too, and she would bestow her smiles freely, promising to meet them all again. This made John angry so he took her away to a seat under the city wall where the air was still and the stone sheltered the warmth of the sun. When our mother awoke and could not see her daughter, she would be at first alarmed, then angry and always hustle us away.

We made our way back to the High Street to find Uncle Fred waiting to take us back to his farm. We drove down the High Street past St Mary's Church with the idolatrous images of the Virgin and Child over the porch. I tried to hide the fact, even from myself, that I liked them. Soon we were approaching East Bridge and the little Cherwell, two arms of it coming together by the new Physic Garden and then gently flowing to join the Thames. Over the bridge soft hills appeared around us, then the steep Chiltern escarpment showed ahead. To our right was the softer outline of the Berkshire Downs where Saint Birinus preached the Christian faith and walked with King Cynigils to found the Abbey Church of Dorchester.

When we came to the steep little turn that led up to the Eliot Farm Rose would race to meet us, flushed with running, or did she blush? If it was late summer or autumn, we would collect the mushy pears in great bins and Margery would make them into perry which was good, healthy and heady, preferred by some to cider or ale. The smell of the brew is in my nostrils as I write and I see again the great barn full of barley for the malting, the grey stone Church, neighbourly and friendly, and the villagers coming from their cottages to worship, treading the great stone slabs as their ancestors had done before them.

In the spring of 1638, shortly after the Eliots had left Banbury, there was great excitement about a visit to London. My father had business in the cloth market at Blackwell Hall while Fred Eliot had heard of a crop that would both cleanse the soil and provide winter food for his animals. Both men wanted to sense for themselves the growing unrest in the capital. Rose and I could go with them, Robert would stay to manage the business while Hannah would remain at the Eliot farm, the prospect of long days in Oxford to cheer her. We took the bags our mothers had prepared for us and packed cheerfully into the cart that took us to Oxford where we changed on to the London coach at the Mitre in High Street. It took us two days to reach London, for the 'Flying Coach' that would do the journey in a day was not yet in use. The inn at Henley where we spent the night with the twenty other passengers was crowded, and all the more fun for that. We walked down to the Thames and saw it in all its splendour with hungry ducks and haughty swans. But I still preferred the intimacy of the Cherwell and Rose was quite ready to agree with me.

In the evening of the second day, we reached London. As we approached the city the heaps of rotting refuse surprised me There was many an open sewer of filth and we saw men throwing garbage and emptying pails of what looked like dirty water. A stench rose, so much so that some ladies were clutching an orange studded with cloves to their noses. A merchant friend of my father's had provided accommodation for us all in his big house in the city. Little notice was taken of Rose and me as the three men sat late into the night, talking. We saw little of our host, who left very early next morning, save that he was a big, dark man with a great forked beard and a beautiful, deep voice. Rose thought he was 'rather ugly', but I knew not. We believed he must be rich for the house was not only large but grandly furnished, while the table was laden with food more lavish than any I had seen, with venison and beef, swan-roast, comfits and fruits. I heard my father talk of Merchant Venturers and concluded our host was one who would buy bales of cloth from the Sedleys for export.

We sat in the evening by the big open fire, for although the day had been warm, the evening was chilly. While Rose and I made pictures in the fire my father and Uncle Fred joined our host and some other men. Although their talk was low, I understood they were discussing a young Puritan who had evaded the censorship laws to circulate tracts against the bishops. He had defied the Court of Star Chamber who tried his case and for his double offence was imprisoned in the Fleet prison. Now, it seemed, he was about to receive further punishment. That was the first time I heard the name of John Lilburne, 'Freeborn John' they called him because of his defiance as a 'free-born Englishman'. My blood tingled with excitement as I jumped up. 'What will they do to him?' I asked. The question took the men by surprise as they had not seen us sitting by the fire. Our host came over and with a sigh said,

'He'll be whipped at the cart's tail from Fleet Street to Westminster where he'll stand in the pillory 'til he can stand no longer. They'll tie his hands to the back of a cart. The cart will pull him slowly and a man with a whip will strike him as he walks, over and over again. He'll start near here from Ludgate.'

My father hesitated for a moment then turned to Rose and me.

'You must watch. You should know what is done in the name of the Church and of the King.'

I looked up at the picture of King Charles on the wall. It was as I remembered him from years before, a handsome face but sad, looking with a little smile at his wife with his children round his knee. It was not a cruel face, rather was it gentle. He was bound to be imperious, everyone expected him to be so. I said as much to the men.

'The King,' said our host, 'is not a bad King. He is led by evil counsellors, by an Archbishop who makes our English Church a Popist replica and by ministers who encourage him to levy taxes of his own will.'

'Like ship money!' I exclaimed, proud of my knowledge.

'The boy learns quickly,' said our host, and the

men laughed.

The next day, early in the morning, we were taken through streets already thronged with people, to Fleet Street where the Fleet Prison was pointed out to us, through Temple Bar and into the Strand. On the south side of this street the mansions of the rich and powerful looked down upon the River Thames. Buckingham had had a house here. Did his widow still live there, I wondered? The houses on the north side were grand enough in our eyes, though perhaps not mansions, and it was into one of these that we were led and taken to an upper room with windows looking onto the Strand. The April day was warm and sunny, the tall windows were open and we made our way through the little crowd gathered there to peer down into the street. Time passed quickly enough and soon the Strand was lined with people on either side. Rose was disappointed with the women's dress declaring London women were not so grand as Oxford folk.

'I expect these are not the grand people, just ordinary people. I suppose they wouldn't wear their best clothes on a day like this. Why would they want to celebrate?'

'Perhaps they DO celebrate,' said a tall man standing behind us. 'This is the beginning… Now at last the game's afoot!'

I turned in amazement. The voice, Shakespeare, the Player King… But the man had gone.

But now, distinct from the voices in the room, there was a distant hum, growing to a roar. A girl with long golden hair streaming behind her rushed into the room, pushing her way through the group by the window, breathless with running.

'He's coming! He's coming! Shouting Glory, Hallelujah, and all the people flock.'

The story of what I saw with Rose when we were so young has been told many times, passed on from mouth to mouth, described in pamphlet after pamphlet, recounted in the newssheets. But my own recollections are still to me more vivid than the words of others, even those of Freeborn John himself.

I stood with Rose by the tall window of the house in the Strand looking down on a street lined deeply with people on either side. They were strewing rosemary and bay in his path. Slowly the cart came into view, the horse that pulled it ambling along, happy perhaps not to be straining at some heavy load, little knowing that the slower he went the longer the agony of the young man in his wake. The crowd was quieter now but as the young man came into full view the crowd groaned. Such a sound of anguish and resentment I had never heard before, and only once since. Tied to the empty cart by his wrists, his arms extended to the full, his back bent, slowly walked a young man clad in nothing but his breeches and boots, his pace determined by the pace of the slow-stepping horse. The gaoler, immediately behind his charge, was whipping him cruelly every three or four paces with a three-thonged, corded whip. The great weals showed upon his back, the blood splayed upon the ground.

From time to time Lilburne managed to raise his head and address the onlookers. As he passed the balcony where we stood, he appeared to look straight up at us and I saw for the first time the handsome features of a young man not much older than myself, in the grip of pain and ecstasy. Jesus, I thought, would have had the same appearance of elation, of conviction, of suffering. But the people had jeered Jesus. Now they were crying 'Be of good cheer! God be with you!' And Lilburne replied:

'Glory Hallelujah! Glory, honour and praise to thee O Lord for ever.'

The girl with golden hair pushed her way out of the room and in the frenzy of the moment Rose and I followed, unnoticed by our parents. We followed her closely, keeping pace with the procession now almost hemmed in by the people. Mounted soldiers were lining the route, pressing back the crowds who got too close. We followed down Whitehall and into Palace Yard where the pillory stood.

'Five hundred blows, three times five hundred stripes,' murmured a voice at my elbow.

'Will they dress his wounds?' asked Rose. The other shook his head.

'Pity shall blow the horrid deed in every eye,' he whispered as he made his way from the crowd.

It was hot for April and from the front of the crowd we could see that Lilburne was dripping with sweat as well as with blood. As his hands were untied and he was released from the cart he collapsed and fell. It was not clear what happened next. A man in uniform it seemed was talking to him while Lilburne was shaking his head. 'Offering remission of the pillory no doubt, if he'll retract,' a man murmured.

It was clear that Lilburne did not retract for he was dragged to the pillory where he was forced to stoop and put his head in the hole. He was quite tall in stature and the pillory was too small for him. The sun was hot in the sky, he was without a hat, his wounds were still undressed and we could see the bloody weals and the great swellings caused by the bruises from the knotted whip.

Lilburne started to talk and the crowd fell silent.

He told the story of his arrest and began a violent attack upon the bishops who, he said, derived their authority from the Pope, the great anti-Christ. The crowd roared their approval. A man stepped forward and bade Lilburne be silent. When he refused, they gagged him, so roughly that the blood spurted from his mouth and ran down his chin. Undaunted, Lilburne stamped his feet and drew papers from his breeches pockets which he threw towards the crowd. Many darted forward to pick them up, as did I. Some dipped their handkerchief in the blood that stood in little pools around.

The tumult now was considerable, with soldiers and officers trying to clear the crowds and confiscate the papers Lilburne had thrown down. A grave young woman I had noticed walking all the way by the cart now darted round the guards for a moment or two and wiped the blood from his face. They seemed to exchange a few words before the soldiers dragged her away and I saw a smile on Lilburne's lips.

Tears were streaming down Rose's cheeks and she wondered what they would do to him.

'Take him back to the Fleet,' said a voice behind us. 'They'll not release him now but we'll make good use of him.'

It was our host of the great forked beard. In spite

of what seemed to be disregard for Lilburne's suffering his voice was full of compassion. I felt respect for our host even in that brief encounter and saw how he pushed his way through the crowd with an air of authority. 'Lucy will bring you back,' he called over his shoulder. And so, the girl with long golden hair stepped forward. She told us our host was her uncle, her mother's brother. When we asked who he was she seemed surprised. 'He's William Walwyn, the most important man in the city of London.' She told us he was a Merchant Adventurer, very rich, and also the writer of books, maybe they were against the Bishops. Then as the streets became less crowded Lucy spoke about 'the cause' which seemed to mean fighting bishops and ship money and taxation and everything the King did when Parliament was not sitting. She was confiding but mysterious about being 'called upon to help'.

'Perhaps my uncle will ask you to help too,' she said.

5

There was much coming and going in the merchant's house that evening, and while we sat alone by the fire making pictures from the shapes of the burning logs, there was a constant sound of feet, of doors opening and shutting, and of voices. When at last the door of the big sitting room opened my father and Uncle Fred were there with the merchant and the lady we had seen by the pillory.

'Elizabeth here,' said Walwyn, 'has a plan for getting pen and paper to Lilburne in the Fleet Prison and for getting out his written pages too. Your father and your uncle are of our counsel and vouch you can be secret and quick-witted too. It is both these qualities will be required.'

I protested I could, indeed, keep a secret and was wondering whether to acknowledge quick-wittedness or to be more modest, but the merchant was continuing.

'Tomorrow they'll allow a surgeon to dress his wounds. The surgeon needs a boy to carry medication, to fetch water if necessary. His boy will be sick tomorrow and you will take his place.'

I felt the blood rush to my face with pleasure, apprehension and disbelief. But Walwyn was speaking still.

'You will wait here tomorrow and I will instruct you.'

Full of wonder I returned to Rose by the big fire and shortly after the grown-ups left. As she was going, Elizabeth put her hand on my shoulder. I saw then how young she was, perhaps eighteen or nineteen.

'Be of good cheer,' she said. 'We will not forget you. The Cause is good.'

At first light next day I was roused by Walwyn himself and told not to dress in my own clothes. Instead, I was provided with garments more suited to a surgeon's boy and given fresh bread and milk.

'Eat lad!' commanded the merchant. 'You will need stamina before the day is out.'

'Now,' said Walwyn, coming to sit beside me, 'you'll stand in for Dick Davey, the apothecary's boy, who usually accompanies the surgeon. Today he is sick.'

I nodded. 'But what am I called?'

'You keep your own name. But what you must remember is the names of the liniments and salves the surgeon calls for. You must be prepared to take the bowl and find water, or else to let the gaoler find it for you. You must use your wits. We cannot foresee the gaoler's mind and you must suit your actions to his. These are the boxes and bottles you'll need to know: an ointment of St John's wort, oil of dill, juice of wood sorrel, gentian steeped in wine, decoction of agrimony, maybe distilled parsley water.'

He lifted each little container lovingly as he showed them to me, as though relishing the healing properties of each common plant.

I, indeed, knew them all and where they grew. To give the right name to each strange-looking concoction was more difficult. But Walwyn's very presence gave me confidence as he went through the names again and I was satisfied that my own good memory would not fail me. Then I learned how to undo and do up the bag and to sling it over my shoulder. Lastly, I was given a small, round bowl in which to get water.

'Now,' said Walwyn, 'this is your calling. This is where you need all your wits for you face risk, both to you and John Lilburne.' He took a small packet of writing material. 'This must be secreted quietly in the cell. Only you and he will know where you put it.'

'But… isn't the surgeon sure to see?'

'The surgeon is an old man. He doesn't see well. He will be intent on the prisoner's wounds which, in all conscience, are severe enough. Besides, he's not unsympathetic to us and would not pry too deeply into your movements. It's the warders you'll have most to fear. But, unless he goes of his own choosing, there'll be a moment when the prison officer in the room will be called away. Act then.'

In the inner, secret lining of the apothecary's bag the papers were hidden, the shapes of the bottles and jars obscuring their bulk. We walked a little way to the surgeon's house where Walwyn left me. The surgeon and I then made our way to where the Fleet river flowed, evil-smelling, choked with garbage and the overflow of privies. What a contrast to sweet Cherwell! The gaol was built over the noisome stream and with many twists and turns we made our way to what must surely be the inmost cell of that foul prison. With great ceremony the gaoler clanged his keys, doubtful if they would fit the lock. His face was pallid as though he too were a prisoner, never leaving that loathsome place. He made it seem he did not have the right key and would leave us there but the old surgeon, for all his age and infirmity, was commanding.

'Open that door at once,' he demanded. 'If the prisoner is dead already of his wounds the blame is yours alone.'

With a leer the gaoler pulled out another key from his breeches pocket and the door creaked open.

At first, I could see nothing. But faint sounds guided my gaze to a pile of rags in one corner and I followed the surgeon to that spot. There lay the young man I had seen taking the cruel punishment only but yesterday. He was tossing to and fro as though he could find no comfort in any position and was murmuring a prayer or poem to himself:

'… Thou art my fort, my sure defence, my Saviour and my King…'

As we approached his filthy makeshift bed, he heard us and opened his eyes, fear and defiance rushing across his face.

'I've come to dress your wounds my friend,' said the surgeon softly. 'God in heaven, never have I seen a back so sorely lacerated!'

'Praise God,' murmured Lilburne, 'for I am in sore pain.'

I was hanging back, scarce able to look upon the prisoner in his torment. The gaoler was gazing, it seemed to me with pleasure, at the sight. I remembered my lesson well and produced with speed the salves and ointments that the surgeon demanded, laying them before him on the filthy blankets. When he called for water the gaoler laughed 'You won't get water here' and I thought I saw a glimpse of malice in his eyes.

'Water!' demanded the surgeon again, 'or I won't be responsible for the prisoner's life and you, my man, will pay the price!'

Sulkily then the gaoler took the bowl from me and with a clang of his keys left the cell. I quickly approached the bed, for the gaoler could not have played more neatly into my hands. I thought I saw a gleam of recognition in the surgeon's eyes but I remembered Walwyn's words: 'It depends on you alone, use your wits…' My hand went quickly inside the lining of the apothecaries' bag and I knew that John Lilburne saw me as I slipped the packet under the ragged bedclothes, for he immediately changed his position so that he was lying on it. To my amazement then there was something in the prisoner's hand. I obeyed my instinct and took it, hiding it in my bag. All this while the surgeon was examining the weals and exclaiming that they were the biggest and most cruel he had ever seen. When the gaoler returned with the water, he washed the wounds and applied balm, calling for more water to wash the filth from the bedclothes.

It was a blessed relief when we stood outside the prison gates, though even here the air was foul from the Fleet stream. It was a place for rats, the messengers of death. Back in the quiet of Walwyn's house I found I was trembling; I could scarcely stand. But in the prison my resolve had been steadfast, I had known what I had to do.

There were many questions, all of which I answered truthfully. Yes, I had delivered the writing material and Yes, John Lilburne had seen it. I told them how he turned so that his body hid it beneath his blankets. My fingers were tightly holding the packet I had been given and when I showed it to them there was excitement in the room. Elizabeth made to take it but Walwyn was first. He opened it and read.

'A Worke of the Beaste. A relation of the most unchristian censure executed upon John Lilburne the 18th of April 1638 with the heavenly speech uttered by him at the time of his suffering....'

Tears were in Elizabeth's eyes as Walwyn spoke.

'This will be printed and distributed up and down the streets of London by tomorrow's nightfall.'

And he went over to his big desk and began to read, marking the paper every now and then with his quill pen.

I quietly left the room to find my father coming down the stairs followed by Rose and Uncle Fred. We were to depart on the Oxford coach at noon. I could hardly believe it was still so early. Little was said as I packed my bag but I like to think there was a gleam of pride in my father's eyes for his son, satisfaction too. I could think only of the young man, in pain and squalor, writing his pamphlets. Years would pass before I met with him again but the words written from that prison cell stay with me.

'I will, come life, come death, speake my minde freely and courageously.'

A man, suffering pain and fearing he was being left to die, indignant and rebellious, had the strength to tell his mind to the world. I see again the dungeon and smell the decay and wonder how I, a boy scarce out of school, was able to be part of this big rising.

Back at home there was an atmosphere of intrigue unknown to me before. Was it new or was my understanding heightened by my meeting with Lilburne? Broughton was the centre of this rising and from there currents were running throughout the Midlands. I felt their impact and waited, as my father and Robert were waiting, for the spark that would ignite them. There were many visitors to the Sedley home where talk went on in my father's office far into the night. Of the family, apart from my father, only Robert was always present. I would watch the arrivals from the window. Even after dark I could distinguish

Uncle Fred and several Banbury men. I knew the sharp voice of Lord Saye and Sele. The horseman my father came out to greet was surely none other than our distant kinsman, John Hampden, from Buckinghamshire.

I asked Robert once to tell me what they came for, what they talked about. Were they planning some enterprise? After my visit to Lilburne in the Fleet I felt it was only right that I should be part of any conspiracy.

'The Scots,' said Robert, 'will fight the King for their religion and a Scottish war will help our cause. We'll have a Parliament soon, you'll see! A Parliament after ten years without one. Why, ye'll not even remember what a Parliament is!' His hand slapped my back with force and affection.

After a while there were fewer meetings at the Sedley home and attention moved more surely to Broughton. There, I feel, is where it all began. Many a time I would be called on to go with Robert to the old woad mill to lead the men who gathered there to the secret passage that led to the Castle. Here, at its entrance, by the couch of bracken which John had made for Hannah, Nathaniel Fiennes would take over and lead the conspirators, for such they surely were, into the castle. I never learned where the passage led or what the men did who used it. But many of them arrived begrimed and fatigued as though they had ridden far. John Hampden was one of them, another surely Lord Brooke, and the burley, thick-set man could well have been John Pym.

In those summers of increasing uncertainty Rose and I were much together for she stayed with us while her father sped between Banbury and Oxford. The easy intimacy of our youth continued while we were half afraid of the intrigue around us yet glad to be part of it. I wanted to tell her how much I loved her but the uncertainty of conflict made me pause. And perhaps our early intimacy of brother and sister stood in the way of a different relationship. Rose was so used to being guided by me that when I didn't lead, she was as lost as I was. So we continued much as before, except that we were now man and woman and not boy and girl. We took the old boat out on the Cherwell, rode fast and long, talking at times about my future. If war was to come my future as a commoner at Cambridge became uncertain. We found Ezekiel one day on the common, all his old buoyancy gone.

'War's not for us,' he said, 'one side or t'other, war's all the same.' The next day the gypsies were gone.

Will Cherwell came often to our house in those days and Hannah would go often to old Sarah's cottage. Now there was little talk of witchcraft. 'If it's war we'll need all of these,' he said as she pointed at her potions and salves. And she would send us out to collect the herbs and flowers that she needed, knowing well enough where they grew and when they were at their best. We took her cowslip, heartsease, herb Robert and hyssop. She sent us down to where the hens were kept for sage, thyme, rosemary and lavender. She knew when to use the roots, the head or the stalk. Those days collecting plants were the last peaceful days we knew.

Events were moving quickly with one Parliament after another summoned for 1640 and two of the Fiennes brothers riding to London to represent us, James for Oxfordshire and Nathaniel for Banbury. They released John Lilburne and other prisoners for conscience sake but King and Parliament could not agree. There was unease all around. The merchants, grim and tense, paced about Banbury thinking of their balance sheets while the weavers in their cottages would ask 'War? They say there's to be a war?' They knew too well what war would mean to them. I could only shake my head. We had a Parliament now, wasn't that enough?

The drift into war was slow, an unthinkable war between King and Parliament. There was drilling in the fields outside Banbury, old muskets brought down from the attic. We tried to follow a drill manual with the men from the cloth mill and the weavers who came in from their cottages. Hannah exchanged her petticoat for male attire but was instantly recognised and sent home by Robert. 'There'll be women enough at the wars,' she murmured, hanging her pretty head to hide her tears. I was now nearly eighteen and could not be excluded. It was Robert who took charge and though no scholar he understood the drill manuals instantly. With his burly figure and loud voice, he brought us into some degree of order. We found ourselves part of an army under Lord General Essex and were kept together under Captain Nathaniel Fiennes. Many had been issued with the blue coat of Lord Saye and Sele as well as with the orange sash of Parliament while we, the Sedley family at least, were well mounted. I was proud of my blue coat, proud that Salvatrice, my favourite horse, was now really mine. What greater bond could there be between man and horse than to do battle together.

It was my father who spoke to our little company after the King had raised his standard at Nottingham and war was inevitable.

'My friends, we have all – you and I and your sons and my sons – left our trades and callings to fight a just war. The conflict is not of our making. We have lived too long with the dove of peace to welcome the eagle of war. But we cannot live at ease in such a time as this. Our religion is thwarted, we are persecuted for speaking or writing the truth as we believe it, we are taxed by the arbitrary power of a king. Our only hope my friends, my neighbours, my workers, lies in the Parliament we have elected but which the King spurns. It is under the banner of that free Parliament that we fight. We expect neither ease nor comfort, neither quiet days nor peaceful nights, but our goal is clear. We fight to end the tyranny of a King's prerogative, we fight that freedom may flow like a mighty torrent to water the land we love, made barren by arbitrary rule.'

As the cheering died down my father cried, 'God be with you. May He help us to endure what is to come, may He guide us to victory in a just war, may He bring us to a just peace for the benefit of all and for His Name's sake!'

I had never heard my father speak like this. Drawn up behind him as he spoke stood the families of these working men called upon to exchange the implements of peace for the weapons of war. My mother and Hannah were among them and I saw how they held their heads high and proudly in support of the cloth merchant turned soldier. It was afterwards that I saw the bitter tears my mother shed. Now there was little time for sentiment. The last farewells were said and we were part of an army marching and riding west from Banbury.

I had said my farewell to Rose the day before. Transport between Banbury and Oxford could well become difficult (how difficult we did not know at the time) and Rose, it was thought, would be better with her mother. So, Rose and I had said 'Godspeed', though nothing in my life had prepared me for this. I had confused ideas that I might die and this was the last time I would see her. We kissed as we always did and I felt Rose might have been wanting a more tender farewell. I wanted to say, 'When this war's over, we'll be together always…' But all I said was, 'Rose!' Our farewell was brief but that was my fault. No more was said.

6

THE WORLD TURNED UPSIDE DOWN

My first days as a soldier were spent in mud, the legacy of the wet September of 1642 and the poor condition of the roads of England. There was mud and deep ruts into which my horse sank to the knees. Poor Salvatrice! I felt for her more than for myself. She was a young mare but already there was an affinity between us and I did all I could to guide her round the deepest ruts, to keep her from the thickest mud. Around us horses were sinking to their flanks while gun-carriages were bogged down with insufficient draft animals to free them,

There was the constant cry for horses, for oxen, for carts, for wagons, as parties of men were sent to farm after farm to secure more. We spent nights in barns and outhouses, sometimes more fortunately in the warm kitchens of houses where we quartered. We had little but the regulation army food, a mere pound of baked bread or biscuit and half a pound of cheese a day. We were fighting a war and soon learned that the King was making for Shrewsbury and that our task was to come between him and London.

We, the Sedleys, were with the party of horse and dragoons which was sent forward under Captain Fiennes. Such a baptism of fire did we receive that day, though not in the manner we expected. When we left the shelter afforded by the little River Teme and the bridge at Powick we were obliged to advance along a narrow lane towards fields to the south of Worcester. We knew the Royalists were torching houses and pillaging 'the sturdy soul of freedom', but the sight of Prince Rupert took us by surprise. We had not experience enough to resist the terrifying onrush of Rupert and his cavalry. In the narrow lane, flanked by high hedges, we had no room to move, nowhere to go but forwards or backwards. I heard my father's voice, but what he said I could not hear. It must go down to our credit that we did not panic but after a short resistance, further confused by orders we could barely hear, still less understand, our little force fled. Robert, and I was there by his side, sought to continue the fight but we were swept along by the rest. Not until we reached Pershore nine miles away were we able to draw rein. Several of our number were killed, three or four of my father's men were taken prisoner, an officer was seen to fall, sore wounded, and to be carried away.

When we re-joined the main army the men were shaken but, as one of them remarked 'We know now what war is like.' They talked about the day and Robert was angry.

'Our intelligence was at fault. We thought to have taken them in the rear. We were at fault to venture into a lane where there was no room to fight… We couldn't hear the word of command… The great black devil who led them was surely Prince Rupert.'

It was a moment or two before my father replied.

'That indeed was Prince Rupert. His men are seasoned troopers who have been fighting in Europe since before some of you were born. No, we've nought to be ashamed of lads. We know something of war now. We'll know Prince Rupert next time we see him!'

Our spirits were further restored when we realised we were riding back towards home and Banbury, little knowing what lay ahead. Looking back, it seems that no-one knew, not even our commanders, what lay ahead. We believed we were still trying to prevent the King from returning to London, but where he was, was uncertain. There was something strange about that time as we floundered on from Worcester to Warwick not knowing where the Royalist army lay. Some of the men would start up in the night, swearing they heard the hooves of cavalry or the preliminary shots of battle. Some slipped away in the darkness, our Intelligence too rudimentary to detect them. For some the strain was too much for action and they lay inert. The greatest cohesion lay with the men of my own troop who were quartered together and knew each other as neighbours. With the rest of the army there was little contact until suddenly the enterprise became real as we reached the little town of Kineton where Rose and I had dallied on many a market day. There the word went round that the King was between us and Banbury, that he was planning to take the town and that Lord General Essex would seek battle with him here, before Kineton. We knew

Essex could rely on the trust and obedience of his officers and his command was undivided as he got his forces into position.

It was dawn on a clear autumn day when we came to position in the Vale of Red Horse, our backs towards Kineton facing the open country that ends in the ridge of Edgehill. As we waited, the first Royalist troops appeared on the hill. Hour after hour we watched the numbers grow. Towards noon we made out the King, a black cloak covering his armour, riding along the ranks with a great red banner borne before him. The two little figures who accompanied him were surely the young Princes. The sound of distant cheering came through the still air.

The plain where the Parliamentarian army watched and waited was a sea of faces, old and young, tough and experienced after serving in foreign wars, smooth and expectant, some frightened perhaps like the boy next to me. Up there on the ridge more Englishmen were gathered. I had time to wonder why I was in the plain and not on the hill. I wondered how I would distinguish one from another and fingered my orange-tawny sash to give me confidence. Chaplains came down the line speaking of God or the Lord or Victory. The man next to me seemed to groan or cry out. I myself was aware of my stomach protesting for want of food. Then there was a rider with an orange-tawny scarf riding out over the plain towards the Royalist position. At first, we thought the battle was begun but there was no word of command and soon we saw the rider tearing off his scarf and riding without hindrance towards the Royalist cavalry. He was followed by other troopers and the ground between the two forces was littered with colour. These desertions did more than anything else had done to stiffen the men and a low murmur of disgust followed by determination rose from the ranks.

It was well after midday when the colours on the hill began to move slowly, it seemed, down into the plain. There were shouts of command from our own captains and the battle was joined. We could see them, on the enemy's right wing, a cavalry charge down the hill that must surely wipe out all before it. The horsemen cut through Parliament's left wing as through a field of standing corn. There was no time for thought. A brief mixing of red and orange sashes and then, on Parliament's right wing, I could see no more as I concentrated on the difficult, soggy ground, with Salvatrice stumbling in the ruts and ditches, neighing in bewilderment and fright while the field of battle was rapidly obscured by the powder and smoke of the guns. We fought on in semi-darkness, sometimes obeying a shout of command, sometimes answering an appeal for help, breaking, re-forming, pushing forward, giving way, joining a cavalry charge. We lurched over bodies amid cries of encouragement or of pain and the terrified neighing and stampeding of horses.

Men were reeling like drunkards, a blow in the thigh unseated me and when I struggled to my feet there was no sign of Salvatrice. There was no escape, little feeling of victory or defeat, but gradually an easement, a slowing down, an ending. It was then I saw the officer in the purple colours of Lord Brooke. It was four years since I had seen him, but there was no mistaking the face. Then he was ill, ragged, unkempt, marked with pain and suffering. Now he was flourishing his musket and shouting.

'One charge more! One charge more and we have them!'

But the carnage was thick upon the ground and I, like other sons, was seeking my father among the dead and wounded. I shouted across to Lilburne.

'John Lilburne! John Lilburne! Doesn't remember the boy in the Fleet prison?' Lilburne heard his name over the noise and confusion, caught the reference to the Fleet and we stumbled towards each other.

'I seek my father, John Sedley.'

'Many on either side seek their parents or their sons. Yonder Lindsay's son stands guard over his sorely wounded father. None of us would grudge him such poor comfort.'

Some remnants of the battle at that moment surged towards us. We stood back-to-back, Lilburne and I, holding the enemy at bay, he shouting out loud for his men who came at last to beat back the cavaliers. Night was now falling and Lilburne had taken charge.

'We will not desert the field,' he declared. 'You, Sedley, seek your father while there is yet light enough to see.'

I sought among the living and the dead, those whose wounds cried out for succour, those beyond all mortal aid. I kept saying to myself that a faithful son will always find his father.

When I found him, he was crouched over Robert who, though conscious still, was unable to move for the great gash in his side from which the blood was pouring. 'A gunshot wound,' murmured my father as he bent over his wounded son. 'We'll get you home, Robert.'

Fires were springing to life as both sides prepared to keep the field. Only a desultory shot or two broke in on the subdued babble of men's voices, the neighing of horses, the moaning, sometimes rising to a shriek, of the wounded. By good fortune Lilburne was there again. He had water which he held to Robert's lips. With some of his men he had commandeered a cart drawn by a couple of horses on which already lay several wounded men. Robert was carefully raised and placed beside them but he lost consciousness as they tried to staunch his wound.

'To Kineton!' cried Lilburne. 'There are field hospitals there and the people are opening their houses to the wounded. We'd never get your brother the ten miles to Banbury,' he explained to me.

We knew this was true. Our horses were lost in the battle and together my father and I trudged by the cart the three or four miles to Kineton, stumbling in the darkness over the dead and wounded. The cart could take no more as it swayed over the rutted ground now hard and slippery with frost. We felt each jolt more for the wounded men in the cart than for ourselves. Every now and then, when a flare cast its eerie light over our little procession, we saw the still, pallid countenance of Robert.

'The sleeping and the dead are but as pictures,' I kept saying to myself. 'Nothing of this is real.'

We reached Kineton while the night was still dark

and cold. But the doors of the houses stood wide open and there were lights within and without. We saw the carts and wagons of the Parliamentary baggage train in the disorder left by Rupert's horsemen after the mad onslaught of the battle, their contents strewn over the streets of the little town.

In one of the bigger houses a surgeon was at work in a ground floor room and Robert was lifted carefully down and placed on a rough couch. As dawn was breaking the surgeon came to him and thrust a finger into the wound to find the direction the bullet had taken. I rushed outside and closed my ears; my brother's pain was too much for me to hear. Only then did I notice my own wound, a sword-thrust in the thigh on which the blood had congealed during the cold night, so saving me from bleeding to death and making possible the walk to Kineton from the battlefield.

We got Robert home the next day, I lying beside him in the jolting cart. He smiled at the familiar faces round him, but his look sent a chill through us all. The gangrene in the wound could not be stemmed, it whipped through him, turning the wound to a greyish-green mush and Robert into a fevered, dying wreck.

As we stood by his bedside, I saw my mother's face, the creasing between the eyes that had not been there before, the quivering of mouth and chin that took the place of tears. She shook off the arm that my father made to put round her shoulders. She would take no comfort, there was none for anyone to give, she would mourn alone. I never heard her speak of 'The Cause' again.

With Hannah it was different. She never left Robert's bedside after we brought him home. When she rose to her feet after a torrent of weeping, she had only one thing to say.

'I will never desert the Cause that HE died for..'

I felt the guilt upon my own shoulders. It should have been me. Why hadn't I saved Robert? Kept close to him in the battle, shielded him from the musket wound, taken it myself. 'Anthony Sedley, trooper, died of wounds received in battle outside Kineton.' That would not have mattered so much, not as much as this.

We buried Robert like a soldier, all of us pacing slowly behind the coffin to the grave, the saddles of the horses covered in black. Robert's mount had not been found though many men had scoured the countryside. Nor had my father's. Only Salvatrice had been brought home, frightened and hungry but otherwise unharmed. Again I felt the guilt that my horse had been found and not the others'.

7

The battle of Edgehill sobered us. We learnt later that the Royalists had been hungry, their tempers breaking. After the King's Standard was taken Lord General Essex claimed victory, but it seemed not so to us as the Royalists were on a clear road to London and would likely take the city. My father had but fatigue and grief to recover from but it would be weeks before my wounded leg would let me move freely. I would have abandoned the struggle then and there had it not been for Robert. But Robert's death did more to stiffen my resolve than all the propaganda which poured from Parliament. Robert had given his life for a cause. I, his brother, could do no less.

After Edgehill, Essex marched off leaving the King to take Broughton and to occupy Banbury. From our home just outside the town we watched the flames. Leaving a garrison there the King marched south to establish winter quarters at Oxford, but we heard he was repulsed when he attempted to enter London. We all thought of the Eliots so close to Oxford. My father, who had been given leave to bury his son and set his house in order, prepared to join

Lord Brooke in London. I cursed my wound and was obliged to learn patience.

My father had to leave the women of the house with some means of defence, so he invited his workmen to move into the big house: Ralph Sowerby, staunch and true, who checked and marked the bales of cloth for London, a widower with sons at the wars, kept at home by his club foot; William Digges, who kept the accounts, through whose fingers, my father would say, ran all the Sedley profits but never a penny piece stuck to them. With the house-servants, the stable boy and the neighbours the family would certainly not be lonely. He gave orders that soldiers must be given what they wanted for this was the surest means of protection both for the house and the household. Lastly, he rode off with my mother to secure provisions.

It was just before my father left that they brought Nan to our house. I remember the day well. I was in the big kitchen with Hannah and one or two of the men. The talk was of whether the war would end soon and whether Rose and I would marry. I was teasing Hannah about young Fiennes but she was so distressed by Robert's death and the war itself, which had caught up so many of the young men we knew, that I ceased to banter. I was seeking to make up for my lack of discernment when they came in. My mother had been crying. My father looked stern.

'Here's Nan. Come to share a home with us,' said my mother.

I stared. It was the strange child from the hidden farm. We hadn't been there for some years and the girl was grown now. But she was still a slight figure, not like a farmer's daughter. Her hair was lank and tangled, as it used to be, she was still dishevelled, her head was bent, her shoulders hunched. I came to know this hunching of her shoulders as though she were cold. She was saying something but she spoke so softly that I had to lean forward to hear.

'They burned our house,' she was saying. 'The soldiers came and took the horses and my brother's gone to fight.'

There was some pride as she told of her brother. Hannah then stepped forward and gently led her off to wash before supper. Only after she had left the room did my mother tell us all.

'They were looking for horses, always more horses, and found some up at Runyon's. Young Dan was there and all the hands. They said they cared not a fig for either side but would go about their own business. One of the soldiers then took Nan and lifted her like a feather, holding her before him on his horse. For fear of what might happen to Nan they yielded horses, carts, fodder, the lot. And so the trooper released Nan, gently enough, Dan said. He was a handsome fellow, old enough to be her father. As they left someone flung a brand at the barn. The handsome trooper cursed him but it was too late. The farm buildings and the house are in ruins. As the soldiers were leaving along comes George Runyon himself. Not seeing his mother or his children but the house in flames he rushes at the handsome trooper to demand where they be and one of the soldiers, fearful of his intentions, shoots him then and there through the head.'

'Dead?' I whispered. 'Dead,' was the reply.

And old Martha, it was too much for her. Seeing the flames in she comes, running from the fields, and falls swooning to the ground never to get up again.

'Dead?' I whispered once more, and 'Dead,' was the reply.

'And young Dan now, mindful only of leaving his sister in good hands, has dismissed his men and they're all swearing they'll be neutral no longer but will go to Oxford and the King.'

It was Dan who had found my parents as they came back from market and taken them to Runyon's.

'Such a sight I never saw!' sighed my mother. She broke off as Nan and Hannah returned, but the picture was clear enough. Both sides were desperate for carts and horses and a neutral farm was fair game for either side.

Nan's first evening in our house was quiet. She went outside and brought in a little black kitten from the yard.

'I want a black one for luck,' she said.

We were suddenly quiet but little Nick broke the silence, chanting.

'Black cats, witches' cats,
Old Ma Trollope in the brambles
In you go and out she rambles.'

She was shy and when I looked full at her for the first time I could see she was still tense and unsmiling, eating little. We were much together in her first days at the Sedley house. As I was waiting for my wound to heal, Nan remained distracted. My mother talked of shock which she said was the same among the weavers who had fought at Edgehill and run away after their first taste of war. Sometimes Nan, slight and pale, would offer her arm as I stumped about the kitchen. As my walking became easier, I asked her if she would come to the river with me, promising to show her the secret places that I knew. She asked me then whether Ma Trollope, of whom Nick had chanted, was a real person.

As I told Nan all I knew of Sarah Trollope the girl grew tense. She had heard of witches who could foretell the future, who could call up spirits so you could talk to them. I had no wish to subject the old lady to a girl's curiosity but Nan was persuasive. I was beginning to realise that, for all her seeming diffidence and gentleness, Nan generally got what she wanted. I remembered the words of her grandmother up at Runyon's farm: 'wilful she is as well as wild.' She had been allowed to keep the little black kitten as her own and take it to her bed, though this was contrary to the rules of the household where cats and kittens had their place in the yard. Nan also kept her hair loose, warding off all attempts to dress it 'seemly' under the linen cap which most of the women wore. She was ready enough to help around the house and with the animals in the yard and for all her seeming frailty she was strong and showed she was accustomed to hard work. But it was on her own terms. She took the horses into her special care and when the mood took her, she would be away for hours on her own, no one knew where, returning windswept, hungry and wet.

'It's the way the child was brought up. She's had a bad time. Give her a little more time,' my mother would murmur.

But Hannah would toss her head and demand what would happen to the house if they all behaved like Nan.

I didn't think too much about it, so when she asked me if I was strong enough to take her to Ma Trollope, I had no objection ready. She told me my leg was healing fast and I should try out my riding. I had no answer to that either, and a few days later I was riding across the common with Nan, as I had so often done with Rose, to the area of low bushes and tangled undergrowth where the old woman, with the help of a man long since disappeared, had built her simple cottage. I was hoping we would see Sarah outside her dwelling, collecting berries or firewood. She was not there so we tethered the horses and Nan knocked on the door. Scarcely waiting for an answer, she lifted the latch and walked in. I thought best to wait outside.

The evening was still and cold. I could hear their voices inside the cottage and saw Nan's dress and figure against the candlelight within. The old lady's voice was rising, more stern than I had heard before.

'I'm no fortune teller, nor do I deal in the future. I

can tell little from the palm of your hand, my dear, but a little more from your face.'

And through the half-open door I saw her take Nan by the shoulders and tip her head back to look at her better.

'And,' she said, releasing her hold on Nan, 'I learn a little more from the questions you ask. When I know you better I will venture more. For the present I have one piece of advice: forget the handsome trooper whose men destroyed your family!'

Her laugh was soft and Nan's reply sombre.

'Good night, mother. May I come again?'

Darkness was closing in as I took Nan's hand to help her through the brambles that were sticking to her skirt. We turned to wave to the old lady but she was nowhere to be seen.

I was aware of a great desire to come closer to Nan. I put my arm protectively round her shoulders to guide her along the path and slipped it lower to her waist. But just then a black shape darted past us, the sounds of evening merging into those of night. There was the sound of the frogs from the pond, the owl's first hoot was loud above us, his second already far away as his great wings took him to his hunting grounds, the cry of an animal in pain pierced the darkness. The human voice was at first part of the orchestration of the night.

Perhaps it echoed Nan's questions of Ma Trollope and at first she did not hear.

'To be or not to be
That is the question....'

She drew closer to me, my protective arm still around her waist as a figure loomed up out of the bushes. The gayness of his manner and his voice could not be mistaken. It was the Player King.

'Whether 'tis better… Isn't that the kind of question you asked old Ma Trollope?' he asked. 'What shall I do? What will my future hold? Do I act? Do I allow events to take a course unaided by me, or do I endeavour to change them?'

He was walking jauntily with us now as we came to the clearing where the horses were tethered. He walked with the slight swagger common to actors, the role of Player King upon him still. He continued.

'Light thickens and the crow
Makes wing to the rocky wood,
Good things of day begin to droop and drowse
Whiles night's black agents to their preys do rouse.'

I relished the words but Nan seemed frightened.

Not knowing what to make of the stranger's words or of his aspect she ran ahead, scrambling onto her horse and making for home. I smothered my vexation and courteously asked the Player King to join us in our supper. He shook his head as he told of Lilburne's capture at Brentford by the Royalists. The burning of Birmingham had given fresh material to the Parliament pamphleteers. They recorded the King's words to Rupert: 'Take their affections rather than their towns', while his persecution and indifference more truly showed his feelings for his rebel subjects. It was important, he said, to release Lilburne, for his influence with the rank and file of Parliament's army was strong. To obtain a Lex Talionis, a threat of reprisals, from Parliament would not be difficult. To get it through the Royalist lines to Oxford was another matter. They had remembered my resourcefulness as a boy four years earlier, they knew I was recovering from a wound, and considered my help was what they needed. I wondered how they knew so much about me and who, indeed, 'they' were. But I remembered Lilburne well enough and, mindful of his help on the battlefield of Edgehill, smarting under my inaction resulting from my wound, anxious to try out my leg in a more testing enterprise than riding with Nan across the common, I agreed to help.

8

ROUNDHEAD TROOPS

The following day, armed with the pass the Player King had provided, I rode south-east from Banbury to keep well clear of Oxford. The countryside was strangely quiet. Some farms appeared deserted, in others I made out a single figure or a few children in the farmyard. Once or twice, indeed, I saw utter ruin with nothing but burnt and twisted timbers to mark the place where a prosperous farm had stood. Few animals were grazing, there was an absence of horses. This was the pleasant, gentle and prosperous country Rose and I had known so well before the war. But even as my thoughts went to Rose, Nan also was there, helping me to walk, riding beside me over the common, close to me as I guided her through the brambles. I brushed such thoughts aside as I approached the Oxford area and became more wary. I gave Islip a wide berth when I made out the figures of horsemen near the village. I forded the little river Ray higher up stream, Salvatrice treading carefully over the stones though recoiling from the cold water. After some consideration I risked going south of Otmore but kept well clear of the rise of Shotover which I knew was a Royalist outpost. I was now in the no-man's land of which the Player King had warned me. Perhaps, I thought, an everyman's land, an any man's land, with Parliament's troops probing north and west from London and Royalist parties making constant sorties from Oxford where the King was firmly entrenched in spite of the Puritan outposts established round the city. If the Royalists made good sport of breaking up these little enclaves the Parliament, for its part, enjoyed the game of infiltrating the Royalist outer defences. What either side would make of an attempt to enter Oxford with a demand from Parliament for the stay of execution upon a Puritan prisoner was not easy to assess.

I considered it more prudent to travel on lanes than on bigger roads, though the mud and the ruts made my progress slow. Close to Waterperry I came across a group of horsemen who were dismounted and stretching their limbs. It took only seconds for me to realise they were Parliament's men, but in that time my blood froze and my hands trembled as I produced the pass which the leader of the group demanded.

'Your destination, Sir?' he asked, 'Your business?'

'My business is with my aunt and cousins,' I answered truthfully enough, 'they live near Oxford and there's been no word since the King's occupation of the city.' I named the Eliots and their farm.

'S'truth, my lad!' exclaimed the trooper, 'we've just come from there.'

Fearing greatly, I asked if all was well and as he looked again at my pass he added:

'Well enough, considering they're between the forces. They'll be all the better for a sight of you! Now, art not with t'army anymore?'

I explained my wound and must needs demonstrate my disability. I was impatient to be off but the men were friendly and sympathetic and took much interest in the great weal in my thigh. None of them had fought at Edgehill so I gave them my account of the battle and the part I played. I did not spare the horror of the encounter.

'The dead and the wounded on both sides were Englishmen, neighbours and cousins, aye brothers and fathers too whether they were called Puritans or Cavaliers, Parliamentarians or Royalists. It mattered little on that morning after battle.'

They took my words soberly. I, indeed, had forgotten everything but that grim aftermath of battle. But one trooper, more aggressive than the rest, approached me.

'Will't fight again? Or art thou one o' them Clubmen without the guts to fight at all?' The others laughed and watched me closely.

'If you've been wounded once and lost a brother in the Cause, you don't give up.'

It was clear my reply was a good one for they let me go at that, instructing me carefully on my route. You could not tell from hour to hour, from day to day where the King would be and where the Parliament would be. But I would be unlucky if I fell in with Prince Rupert, for he was the devil in man's flesh. When mounted he was half as high again as any other man, his reach was longer and more powerful than anyone else's. Robbing and killing were his trade and he feared nothing nor nobody. They talked of him as 'a great black man'. I remembered stories I had heard of Rupert's mother, the King's sister, 'the Queen of hearts', who married her fairy tale Prince in the banqueting hall at Whitehall. Her golden hair was shining, they said, with jewels.

When at last I left them in the dark of a winter's evening I followed their advice and skirted Wheatley, leaving the village to the west and came through Cuddesdon. Lights were shining in the newly finished Bishops' Palace and I had time to wonder who occupied it now. Then down to Denton and up to the Eliot farm. Rose was the first to run out to greet me and there was as much rejoicing as the war allowed, for they had seen none of the family since Edgehill and the terrible death of Robert. Fred Eliot was working hard on the farm, not only to keep his contracts with the city of Oxford and the Colleges but to meet the far greater demands of the King's Court and army for grain, vegetables and fruit, to say nothing of fodder for the horses. At the same time, he told me with a sly smile, he was able to do a bit for Parliament's soldiers as well. I believed that a group of local farmers were working with him, doing what they were compelled to do for the King while not neglecting their own side. Fred was, though, a man worried at what he found himself obliged to do.

'To supply the city, good enough,' he said, 'there's

folk there like us that needs the food. The college demands are small enough but when it comes to the King's army and the King's Court who am I to give comfort and sustenance to our enemies? But it's war and if I refused, they'd burn the lot. There would be no gain for Parliament. Anything might happen at any time. The war swings strangely from one side to the other. Maybe I do Parliament more good by being here.'

From those twisted words I gathered that working his farm was not the only enterprise in which my Uncle was involved. Old Ben, more than ever like a dried-out walnut, still sat in the chimney corner filling the room with tobacco smoke, the look of contentment on his face disturbed at the mention of Robert's name. He was much disturbed by the death of Robert and fearful for the twins who had threatened to disguise their age and join the army in time for the next campaign.

Rose and I took our familiar walk that evening up to the church. The Thames valley was at our feet, the lights strong in Oxford and dim in other hamlets from what might be the scattered outposts of one side or the other. The night was cold and we stood close together in the old familiar way. I had thought that after Edgehill, on some occasion such as this, I would ask Rose to marry me, but I could not ask the question. A dark form darted swiftly by and Rose laughed 'It's the black cat,' but for me there was another voice, 'I want a black one for luck.' I felt again the warm, firm waist my arm had so recently encircled and the question failed to come.

I turned to Rose in my frustration, tired after the long and hazardous ride with my wounded leg. Tormented by my own indecision I pulled her down and found the comfort of her lips, soft as eiderdown. I knew what clothes I needed to undo till I felt her naked body beneath me. My hands found their way to her breasts and ran softly over every part of her body as we lay together on the damp grass by the little church with enemy camps ahead and the scattered Parliamentary outposts around us. My body moved against hers in an ecstasy of pleasure until a feeling of pure peace, unknown to me for so long, came over me. I had no idea what Rose felt, nor did she speak as she made to pull on her clothes. As we returned slowly to the farm my feelings were of bewilderment that after so long it should happen like this.

But there was no time for thought for no sooner had we reached home than riders arrived at the door, one of them none other than Elizabeth Lilburne, now heavy with child. I recognised her as the grave young woman I had met in London five years before. Parliament had demanded a stay of execution upon John Lilburne on pain of reprisal upon a Royalist prisoner. Elizabeth held Parliament's *Lex Talionis* which she was determined to deliver herself to the Royalist judges, for time was short and sentence planned for the following day. If all else failed she thought that her condition might induce pity in the hearts of her husband's captors. So, even though near to her time, she would make the difficult and dangerous journey through enemy lines to the heart of Oxford. The troopers who had accompanied her so far were to return to London and she would complete her journey with me and with Rose who would pass as her brother and sister-in-law. Once inside Oxford, Elizabeth would pass as the wife of a dead Royalist officer anxious to bear her child among people loyal to the King. There was talk as to how we would travel the few miles to the centre of Oxford, whether as Roundheads or Cavaliers. The dangers seemed balanced, for two thousand King's men were encamped around the city while Parliament's men were pushing the whole time. It made me deeply aware of the dangers the Eliots faced. I saw enough to realise that my uncle was turning his position at the edge of Oxford to good advantage to Parliament.

The immediate problem that faced us was did we leave the farm as Roundheads and trust to the help of the landlord at the Swan to let us change into Cavalier costume before we rode further, or did we start as good Cavaliers, trusting we would meet no Roundhead before we reached Oxford? I did, indeed, suggest we might go forward as scholars who had been visiting friends near Oxford, but how could we explain Elizabeth? We talked then of passes. We had good Parliamentarian and Royalist passes, so well prepared that they were unlikely to be questioned. Student passes were another matter. Uncle Fred had the deciding word.

'Well, there may be a couple of thousand King's men hereabouts, but I reckon I know as many Parliament men. Besides, a Parliament man will understand your mission, but what would he say to a group of Cavaliers making for Oxford? Go to the Swan as good Parliamentarians and John Hopgood there will take a note from me and let you rest and change your clothing. But whatever you do, it's tricky.'

The night was for me a turmoil of Rose, Nan, Elizabeth and John Lilburne with the black, menacing figure of Prince Rupert enveloping us all in his long cloak. It was barely dawn when Rose called me. On

Margery's insistence we ate briefly and took with us the change of costume we would need. It was the longest few miles I had ever ridden. I could see Royalist soldiers riding towards Shotover and caught the sound of their refrain.

'Full forty years the royal crown
Hath been his father's and his own,
And is there anyone but he
That in the same should sharer be?
For who better may the sceptre sway?
Than he that hath such right to reign?
Then let's hope for a peace, for the wars will not cease
Till the King enjoys his own again.'

So far, our little group of three had aroused no comment or suspicion. Our cloaks and the early morning mist concealed our uniform as well as our sex. As we approached what must surely be the little village of Cowley and the Swan, my heart took a fresh beat as we heard the sound of soldiers talking. We were as likely to be challenged by one side as the other and we could only go forward in one uniform. I left the two women concealed in the trees when I went forward. Straightaway I knew by the close-cropped hair and clothes of sombre hue that it was a Roundhead

Captain who challenged me and my story was the truth. I told of the message from Parliament to the Chief Justice in Oxford demanding a stay of execution upon John Lilburne and other prisoners held by the Royalists in Oxford Castle. It was more difficult to explain the presence of the women, Elizabeth's condition in particular raising some ribald comments. But they understood and the Captain of the troop spoke to the landlord and delivered my letter from Uncle Fred. No word was spoken but the three of us were shown to a room where we could rest a little and change into clothing more fancy and suited to a Cavalier and his women. But it was Elizabeth, in an agony of apprehension lest we arrive too late, who urged us on. The captain warned us:

'From now on you're in enemy territory. It's enemy country alright. Only your wits will serve you now. Less than three miles now to East Bridge.'

Barely a mile along the road, as we dipped into low-lying marshy land, we perceived a group of horsemen approaching with speed from the direction of Oxford. There was no mistaking the leading figure. We drew into the side of the road hoping in their hurry they would ignore us. But not so Rupert. He reigned his horse sharply, looking with pleasure at the two women while one of his men demanded our business. The story sounded thin as Elizabeth falteringly explained that her husband had been killed at Edgehill and she wished to be with friends in Oxford for her lying-in. But the officers looked at our passes and nodded to the Prince. I, meanwhile, could hardly take my eyes from him with his dark hair, swarthy complexion, nose high and well formed. Our soldiers spoke of 'the tall, black man' with awe, whose charge in battle was irresistible, whose reach was longer than others, the man whose name was on every soldier's lips, who frightened babies in their cradles and children on their mother's knee. I saw an imperious, handsome man, born to command. Son, grandson, nephew of Princes, fighting for a kingdom, for his mother's birthplace, his uncle's realm. What had we to compare with the natural command with which he reigned his horse and addressed us?

I glanced at the three Cavaliers as they surveyed Rose and Elizabeth. Elizabeth was comely, even in her condition and her ill-fitting, borrowed clothes. The cavalier robe and cloak that Rose wore became her well and I saw her gaze was all for the Prince, as it had been for the King and Queen on that far-off day in Enstone. The Prince took her gaze for interest and asked for her name. 'It's Rose,' said one of his companions glancing at our passes. I started forward but met with Elizabeth's beseeching eyes, 'for the love of God remember our mission', and I refrained.

'Ah, Rose,' said the Prince, 'of Lancaster or York?'

His companions joined him in laughing at the pleasantry while he was so close to Rose that his hand touched her thigh. What would have happened then I know not but one of his troopers said something quietly to the Prince who then seemed to recollect himself. Removing his hat, he made a sweeping gesture towards the women.

'Lying-in will not be very comfortable in Oxford but I trust you find your friends. I understand the grief you carry for the death of your husband but take comfort in the justice of the cause for which he died. God rest his soul and God protect his child.'

Then, addressing me directly, he told me I would find soldiers' work in plenty. But his last words were for Rose, looking back over his shoulder.

'Seek me at St John's College or in Christ Church. I'll give you better lodging than your friends will find.' And then they were gone.

I knew Oxford well enough to be able to lead the way to the Court House where the court was sitting. At East Bridge we told our story and produced our passes with a casualness that helped deceive the soldiers who examined them far more closely than

Rupert had done. There was difficulty at first in getting past the guard at the door but I shouted lustily so that my words could be heard inside.

'Important document from the Parliament bearing on the prisoner.'

'Too late!' a voice shouted back. 'Sentence has been passed!'

There was a commotion inside the court room at that and I thought I heard Lilburne's voice. Meanwhile Elizabeth collapsed and Rose was tending her. In the confusion I pushed my way in, holding the paper aloft.

'*Lex Talionis*,' I cried. 'On your own heads be it…'

I reached a position where the judge could see the Parliament's seal on the parchment I was holding. He reached for it over the heads of the spectators and it was passed to him. After no more than a few minutes of consultation he announced a stay of execution upon John Lilburne and the three other prisoners. I thought he seemed glad to do so. It was then that I noticed one of the other prisoners. It was John Vivers, the boy from Banbury, my school friend and one of Hannah's beaux. We waved at each other, relief on our faces, while Lilburne continued gazing towards the door until he saw his wife, leaning heavily upon Rose but smiling and waving to him as though to say, 'We've done it, we've done it.'

Once our papers were accepted and the stay of execution agreed, the Royalists were courteous. They made no comment on the Royalist disguise of professed Parliamentarians but gave us escort to the city gates and safe conduct passes beyond. I had time to regard the old University town in its new guise as Royalist headquarters, home of the King's Court, the seat of his government and the centre of his military operations. Outside St Mary's church I looked for evidence of the shots fired by Lord Saye and Seal's trooper at the image of the Virgin and the infant Saviour. From the narrow opening that led from Sir Thomas Bodley's library, men emerged in full military uniform and we saw men marching in line down the High Street. On East Bridge itself our escort drew to attention, motioning us to do the same as the King himself passed across the bridge from Magdalen tower to the Physic garden. I felt Rose draw close to me, remembering the other time when we had seen the King. Then he had been calm, smiling, debonair. Now he was walking quickly, his face tense and resolute, handsome enough still in his military uniform of Commander-in-chief.

The passes took us to the Swan without trouble. Elizabeth was strangely quiet, her body tired with the weight of child bearing but happy with our success. There, as before, we changed our clothes and emerged as good Parliamentarians. It was now dark as we started our journey home. Many a time we had to draw aside into a coppice while a group of horsemen rode by towards Oxford. When we were nearly there, we heard the sound of a single horseman riding at speed from Oxford in our direction. I stood my ground as the rider approached.

'News! News! Make way for the Mercury Man! No military man am I. I record the news. News of the Court, news of Parliament. If there's a battle I'll tell you about it! I have passes in plenty, from the Parliament, from the King, from the Generals. Take your choice, Sir. I'm the Mercury man, I carry news hot to the printer in London of John Lilburne's court martial in Oxford and his release on a showing of a *Lex Talionis* from Parliament brought, they say, by his wife.'

As he approached close to me, I recognised something in his voice, something in the way he thrust his head forward. It was a boy from Banbury, from my school, my classmate, the humourist of the class.

'Tom Staunton, by all that's holy!'

'Odds… it's Anthony Sedley!' and we embraced with joy and relief.

I told him it was John Lilburne's wife together with two friends who brought the *Lex Talionis*. And so, Elizabeth and Rose stepped forward as I said, 'Come, Tom Mercury, and talk to them yourself.'

9

A great wave of happiness came over me after the reprieve of Lilburne, far different from the despair after Edgehill. There was no opportunity for talk alone with Rose and I said goodbye to her the next day with less emotion than I could have thought possible. If she noticed it she said nothing, and she surely did not notice that my thoughts were racing ahead of me to Banbury.

Nan with young Nick ran to greet me. My mother was in the fields but there was no sign of Hannah.

'She's gone to fight!' announced Nick.

'What! A woman fight?' I asked in disbelief.

'She went with Will Cherwell,' said Nan. 'He's in the army now and when he came to see his mother, he took her back with him.'

'There's several girls from hereabouts gone to join their husbands and follow the army,' my mother continued when she came in. 'They help with food and nursing. Hannah felt alone with so many of her friends gone and now we have Nan she knew I wouldn't be alone. And they're fond of each other, Hannah and Will. It gives me comfort to know he's with her. But she would have gone, for Robert.'

I could see there was little joy in my mother's words, she could see only the confusion of war in those troubled years.

While I had been away Nan had struck up a friendship with Sarah Trollope. The old lady had been lonely since Will joined the army and did not object when Nan lifted the latch and walked in. Her mind was full of strange talk. 'Man's destiny', she told me, 'is read in the stars'. I told her mine was '… thick inlaid with patinas of bright gold'. Rose would have caught the reference, but Nan merely remarked she had not heard what I said.

If only she knew! Suddenly I could not free my thoughts from that other night on the damp grass by the little church. Concern for Rose came over me. Not that I blamed myself for it was an act entered into by both of us, surely our coming together was meant to be. Yet why like this? We were alone, without the sanction of holy wedlock or the blessing of friends and family. And why was I not with her now? Nan was looking at me gravely.

'I told thee, Anthony, about the stars. There's spirits out there, all around us. In the heavens, in the air itself and in the earth. Some are good, many are devils. Does not scripture tell us that the devil possessed the swine? And that men themselves were possessed of devils?'

'The erring angels that fell with Lucifer were not all confined to hell, but some escaped and live scattered, dispersed in the empty regions of the air as thick as motes in the sun… '

This last passage she recited as though it was a passage learned by heart and I asked her, perhaps more brusquely than I intended, what book she had taken it from. I could see the anger in her eyes as the words tumbled out.

'What of elves and goblins in the dairy? The cream, the butter… the dough that won't rise…? These are not fairy tales for children. And what of Mr Shakespeare? He speaks of ghosts, aye and witches too. You, who talk of Shakespeare all the time, who make a master, a God of him, you can't deny that he knew these things.'

She ran inside. How could I explain the playwright's craft to her? Writing for the people of London, for the Court, for himself. Would she ever read the words that transcended anything yet written in the English tongue? Beauty, understanding, knowledge of men – unsurpassed, unsurpassable Will Shakespeare! Would Nan ever know of my dream to study? Yes, I would have gone to Cambridge, not for the reasons my father gave but to follow the great poets. Then there would have been visits to London and the playhouses to see a different company of players each evening. And then the friends and the talk that would have continued all night. But this could never have been. Even before the fighting began the Puritan Parliament had closed the theatres.

'God in heaven!' I cried. 'What am I doing on their side?' I could find no answer as I went into the now sleeping house, grieving as much for the loss of art, poetry, literature, as for my own blighted hopes. Grieving for my first love and for the torment of my new, hating both myself and the cause I was fighting for.

Next morning the house was quieter than I had known it. My mother and Nan were out leaving little Nick, fast growing, to prattle away. The thought came to me that if the war went on long enough, he would be fighting too.

'Tell me about Prince Rupert,' he begged. 'Is he really black and sent from the devil? And what manner of devil is it that goes everywhere with him and fights at his side?'

I was angry with all this talk of the supernatural, but my words were gentle. 'Prince Rupert is a very gallant soldier and a fine commander. The King is his uncle. He fights for him as you would fight for Uncle Fred. And that devil is nought but his little dog, his poodle that he calls Boye, that loves his master.'

'I'd fight for Uncle Fred and for you,' Nick called as he seized a stick and strutted up and down with many a thrust and lunge.

'Pray God it come not to that,' I sighed.

We were sitting around the fire on Christmas Eve when Nick, brandishing a stick and pretending to fight Prince Rupert, came running in, telling us there was a fire in the sky and the stars were falling. As we ran out, we were aware that other people had done the same. The sky to the south west was a suffusion of red, far more intense than the colour of a sunset, and over it dozens of lights like fireworks or flying stars were constantly rising up into the air and then falling. Nan was trembling.

'I told thee Anthony about the stars,' she whispered. 'There's trouble there, trouble for me. The star shoots up and then falls. The red sky means blood. I will find my happiness as the star shoots upward. I will fall in sorrow as the star falls, falls in blood.'

'Perhaps not trouble,' I answered her. 'Perhaps you'll shoot up high in the world, like a bright star, illuminating all around you.'

My mother was angry at what she considered the girl's posturing. 'Such stories you've learnt from those books of yours. 'Tis nought but what we saw ten years ago…'

I remembered the Aurora Borealis, seen over Banbury in 1631 and my spirits rose. Later that night the light appeared again and then the following Saturday and Sunday nights. When stories began to circulate of strange and terrifying occurrences over the battlefield of Edgehill, we began to take more heed. When our old friend the Justice from Kineton came to see us, it was with a story full of wonder and terror. Some claimed to have seen battles so fierce they could smell the gunpowder, others saw flaming swords hanging in the air, to many it seemed like the end of the world. Nothing would keep me from visiting the scene myself and the following Saturday I reached Edgehill. It happened as they had described. First the sound of drums afar off, then getting nearer, horses neighing, men groaning, Then, with the sound of cannon discharging, ghostly figures were visible with their ensigns displayed. They divided into two troops, one displaying the King's colours, the other Parliament's. Dreadful fighting ensued with cries and shrieks of pain, horses and men piling on top of each other. The fury of the incorporeal struggle was cruel. It was then that I became aware of a figure beside me, the voice unmistakeable.

''Tis strange, 'tis passing strange.'

My reply was quick, 'There are more things in heaven and earth, Horatio, than are dreamt of in your philosophy.'

'Bravo,' said the Player King and continued,

'Lamentings heard in the air; strange screams of death
And prophesying with accents terrible
Of dire combustion and confused events
Now hatch'd to the woeful time.'

We rode back to the inn at Kineton together. Here there was great confusion, everyone telling what he had seen and offering some explanation, all gaining courage now that they were back on familiar ground. Two of the King's officers were there, sent to report to the Court at Oxford.

'I tell you,' one of them was saying, 'I saw Sir Edmund Verney plain, with the standard in his hand, and there were others whom I knew.'

'That's true,' I whispered, 'I saw him too, with the standard in his hand.'

I rode home slowly, conscious of the existence of

enormous forces, unknown to man, outside human control. Whether for good or for ill who could tell?

Perhaps I should not have laughed at Nan. Perhaps she really was aware of some world beyond my understanding, some other life I was too stubborn to recognise. As I neared home, I thought of what I had seen. It was similar to the Aurora Borealis and at the scene of Edgehill it had worked upon my imagination disordered by the events of that fearful battle still less than two months past. As for Nan, she was as human as any of us, and I was glad she would be at home to greet me.

Also there to greet us were two soldiers sitting by the fire. The one who rose as I entered was surely Will Cherwell. Old Sarah's son was now handsome, tall and broad with black hair that curled over his ears in spite of frequent attempts to crop it in the Puritan style, and black eyes full of life. Maybe the story that his father was a Spanish nobleman wrecked on our coasts was true. As I began to offer the courtesies of the house to his companion, who seemed weary and had remained seated, the young soldier jumped up and flung his arms around my neck amid laughter all round. For it was none other than Hannah. She had been enrolled as a drummer in Will's regiment and so far escaped detection. Both she and Will wore the purple coats of Lord Brooke's regiment, a good colour, my mother remarked, for both dark and fair. The tight-fitting three-quarter length tunic over sleek breeches with high, close-fitting boots, became Hannah, so I thought, as much as the long full skirts she was always ironing in the old days. I glanced with admiration at my mother, making no fuss as her third child prepared to go to the wars. Her eyes were dry but there was a tightening of the lips I had seen before in times of stress.

Hannah was in high spirits. 'Rat-a-tat-tat,' she mimed. She had seen nothing yet of war but she and Will were on their way to report to Lord Brooke who was now in the Midlands. Just then the sound of the real drum was heard. Will and Hannah jumped to their feet as the door opened to little Nick. He had Hannah's big drum on its long cord slung round his neck and hanging to his feet.

'Bravo!' we all cried while even my mother clapped her hands and Hannah showed him how to hold the drumsticks and how to beat, 'Tra la la la, tra la, tra la.'

It soon became time when I should be with my regiment. Only the winter lull in activities had given me so long a grace. By now my leg was healed and the spring campaign was to begin. My father had not returned so it was my task to leave the house as well provisioned as possible. The household appeared as well provided as I could expect and I went down to the weavers' cottages where Rose and I used to play. I had known my father's people all my life. Weaving with some arable farming and the care of a pig and a cow or two had been their livelihood. Some of them owned a few sheep who grazed in one of the big fields or in grassland round their tofts. Often the girls were at Banbury on market day with their homemade cakes and ale. It was a community that was neither rich nor poor. The shock was great when I saw the difference that a few months had made. I knew that my father's cloth business had suffered in the war and with it the weavers' craft, but I was not prepared for the desolation of the land. There were neither horses nor wagons, neither sign of ploughing nor sowing. Only in the little tofts round their houses did I see signs of cultivation. Most of the men were at the war except for the deserters, the men who had run away and returned home. Most of these were pressed men, not volunteers, who had never thought beyond the loom and the fields until they had been caught up by Militia Ordinance or Commission of Array. For some the shock of battle had been too much. Others had run away from their regiments not through fear but because they judged the needs of their families greater than the cause that either side was fighting for. They showed themselves as little as possible, preparing always to hide if the military appeared. My mother provided food for the weavers, but never enough for a full provision. As I rode home and witnessed the sterile fields I asked myself again, 'Why this?'

My mood changed as I crossed the common by Sarah's house and saw the smoke curling upwards from the dingle. And there, seeming as though they had been living there for weeks, were the gypsies. I galloped towards them, waving my hat in greeting, and sure enough there was Ezekiel, pipe in hand, on the top step of his caravan, his long legs dangling almost to the ground.

'Still polluting the air, my friend, and indeed thy lungs?' I questioned.

'Aye, thanks to Sir Walter. 'Tis one of them silver pipes. I got it down Devon way. Two days' work in fields paid for that pipe. It's good to look at, a pretty thing. But it don't draw proper like the other.'

He showed me how loving hands had polished the engraved silver bowl until it shone brightly with strange markings. That pipe conferred great esteem upon him, though I reckoned it was sure he smoked the other one indoors.

The common was by now alive with people

coming to see the gypsies, and galloping over among them was Nan with little Nick before her. We danced that night, as we always did when the gypsies were there. Nan was like an elfin child as the gypsy men tossed her from dancer to dancer to the wild rhythm of the dance. When she came to me, I found her so light she scarcely needed the touch of my arm to send her twirling to the beat of the tambourines. In her sombre grey, her hair undressed, her head uncovered, she was a strange and fetching contrast to the bronzed and brightly clothed gypsy girls.

As we made our way home Nan spoke of her regret that she had not waited to change her clothes before setting out for the common. She had been afraid they'd go as quickly as they came. We tied our horses together and Nan joined me on Salvatrice. As she pressed close to me, I had not felt happier since the war began. This was a time when there was no right or wrong, only the feeling of her little body against mine, the stars bright in the winter sky and a warm home before us.

10

Next day I followed Will Cherwell and Hannah, who had already left, to report to Lord Brooke who commanded the counties of Warwick and Stafford. He was the owner of Warwick Castle and a staunch Puritan whom I had known and respected all my life. He was a man of wide tolerance and clear intellect, entirely lacking in bigotry. He accepted the war as necessary and threw himself into the fighting. His men had repulsed the King at Brentford, where Lilburne had been taken prisoner, and now he was engaged in driving the Royalists from the Midland counties where they had steadily been gaining ground since Edgehill.

The re-taking of Stratford-upon-Avon was an experience of war that made me feel more seasoned. But it was marred by the consideration that the Royalists would have been better custodians of Shakespeare's birthplace than the Puritans. At Lichfield it was hard to see Puritan cannon directed against the Cathedral, yet as it was a Royalist fortress what else could we do? We re-took Lichfield but a shot from the Cathedral tower ended the life of Lord

Brooke. That sacrifice was too great and I was for throwing down my arms. But Will Cherwell was firm.

'If you stand aside you count for nothing. We began this war to end injustice. Maybe worse things will happen before we succeed, but succeed we must.'

Hannah spoke more fiercely, 'They've killed Lord Brooke and they've killed my brother! I'll follow the army until justice is done.'

'But what is justice?' I cried. 'An eye for an eye and a tooth for a tooth?'

So I remained with the army and marvelled at Hannah. Pretty, frivolous Hannah, ironing her petticoat for one gallant after another, who had taken her baptism of fire better than many a man and who was now as likely a drummer boy as any regiment could wish.

It was not until May that Lilburne was released when he was exchanged for a Royalist of some standing, none other than Captain Smith who had retrieved the royal standard taken from the dead hand of Sir Edmund Verney at Edgehill. In spite of the spring offensive there was time for a happy day on the Thames. The Lilburnes wanted Rose and I to join them. In one of his publications he had called us 'My friends and saviours, without whom my wife, though a gallant female, could never, in her then condition, have reached my tormentors in time to save my life.'

Newly united, John and Elizabeth were like children on holiday. Like many officers John had abandoned the close crop that had earned us the name of Roundhead and his hair, like mine, hung to his shoulders. We pushed the boat out as May blossom showered down on us, the petals spangling Rose's hair as if with stars. I put my arm round her and closed my eyes as she lay close to me in the little boat. But what I might have said, I did not, as Lilburne talked freely of his life, his captivity, the iniquities of the King, of the Bishops and, indeed, of the Parliament.

I was worried there might be a pregnancy for Rose. As we returned from the river, she saw me looking at her skirt which, because of the warmth of the day, she had loosened slightly.

'Nay, Anthony,' she said. 'It was only our loving by the church. There will be none other. And what's one night, one time, when all the world's at odds? I could weep for all the time we've had together, never to be repeated, were not my tears used up in other ways. I grieve not just because you have changed, but for the whole world that's changed.'

So she knew about my feelings for Nan and this

was my dismissal. She had given me freedom to love Nan. I was grateful that she made no demands on me, that she spoke so quietly, yet I felt a pang that she could so calmly dismiss me and all our past. I hardly understood how cruelly I myself appeared to have dismissed that past, while her talk disturbed me. I recalled her clear attraction to Prince Rupert and wondered was she indeed a 'wanton' as the preacher had pronounced her all those years ago. But that thinking brought me no comfort. No comfort came either from thinking of Nan. What was there to attract me in this strange, waif-like creature whose ways were so unlike my own and was as pretty neither as Rose nor Hannah? Likely it was her very strangeness, something of the wildness of the gypsies, some hint of the supernatural that drew me to her.

I was able to make a brief return to Banbury to check on the household and was greeted by Nan who pulled off my boots, took my coat and hat into her care and even removed my sword. That evening, when the moon was full, she cried out to me to ride with her. We stopped by the bushes where as children we had played our mock battles and looked down in the hard, clear light of the moon at the desolate sight of twisted and blackened timbers and earth still scorched. I thought Nan was crying but instead there was a look of exultation on her face that I could not understand.

'He held me there,' she said, pointing, 'before him on his saddle.'

As we rode back like the wind, her hair was streaming behind her. Nothing more was said and she went straight to bed on our return. The following day she busied herself as usual with the house, the kitchen and the farmyard under my mother's watchful eyes.

It was time then to join part of the army under Essex that was pushing towards the King's headquarters at Oxford. Early one morning I was roused to join an attack on Prince Rupert who was raising hell around the Chiltern foothills, looking, so the army scouts reported, for the convoy taking wages to soldiers in Thame. As I joined in the skirmish round the village of Chalgrove I saw that John Hampden was with us. It was I, with one of the troopers, who bore the wounded leader to Thame where his death, the death of one of my childhood heroes, strained my loyalty to the utmost.

I was bitter. There must be a good reason for this fighting. The cause for which we were destroying ourselves must be good. More than that, it must be better than the cause for which the Royalists were destroying themselves. And if right were measured by success the Royalists were right. For there was no denying that through the spring of 1643 they appeared to be winning. I did not know that in the Eastern counties of England a squire named Oliver Cromwell was seeing things in a different way. It was not the cause itself but our attitude to it which was wrong. The easy discipline of our opponents, the spirited yet seemingly effortless determination with which they went into battle must be matched by a similar spirit on the Puritan side.

As troops I and my companions were a ragged band, willing maybe but uneasily brought together by vague ideas of taxation, bishops, poverty and what we termed 'arbitrary government.' Many too had been impressed to fight, though this was common on both sides.

Shortly after the fight at Chalgrove Field I called, with some misgiving, at the Eliot Farm. It was my first visit since the day on the river with the Lilburnes. Rose was not there and her family were worried. Rose had been miserable, restless, they said. The death of Hampden had greatly distressed her. She said she needed to be part of 'the Cause'.

'It's been 'the Cause' this, 'the Cause that', everyone speaks about the Cause. The trouble is you never know what it is. I doubt if they know themselves,' Aunt Margery moaned. 'Where Rose went or what to do, we know not.'

There was much military activity in the neighbourhood and there had been no news of her since she left. Aunt Margery was suspicious of Elizabeth Lilburne, linking Rose's disappearance with the enterprise in retrieving John. Her words became stronger.

'Some of the same soldiers came again to the farm. In the state Rose was in it was an easy matter for them to work on her. It was after that she told us she was going away. And it's my belief she never would have gone if her heart had been here.'

I knew that reproof was for me and I could but take it. With an urgency born of unease I begged her to tell me when she went, where she went, what to do and what she said. Old Ben took up the story.

'Rose was all in tears, no comfort would she take. She was worried and helpless over the war, so are we all. No good will come of the Cause.'

All I could do was promise to search. I had no need of their entreaties to do so, I would search among the troopers of my own regiment, in the villages we passed through, the farmsteads and the Inns. I would search for a girl neither tall nor short, fat nor thin, but brown-haired and pretty for sure. I knew, indeed, of the women who followed the long lines of marching soldiers, whom even the stern discipline of the Puritan commanders could not, or would not, send flying back to the city ghettoes whence they came. Rose could not be among these! But what if she had been taken there against her will, protesting. Then again I heard the preacher's voice in Banbury, 'Get thee gone for a wanton!'. Was Rose a wanton? Was there something about Rose I knew not? I saw again her attraction to Prince Rupert… Perhaps I myself had driven her into the ranks of the camp followers?

Although I had seen little of the army beyond drilling and fighting, I knew how valued was the Commissariat. I knew of the wagons and coaches with the dispatch riders, the representatives of parliament and the foreign observers that followed us, while blacksmiths, farriers, wheelwrights and carpenters marched with us to make immediate repairs to animals and vehicles. I knew that the very household goods of many soldiers, and the wives of even more, made their way behind the marching army. And that with them were the women who were not wives but would serve the purpose. I had heard the laughter and the singing that came at night from this part of the army and knew of men who had crept back from some encounter to seek womanly comfort.

I spoke to one of these men about Rose. For the first time I heard from my own lips how I really considered her.

'In stature a maid neither tall nor short. In colour neither dark nor yet very fair either. Her hair loose, below her shoulders, if it's not caught up in a cap. Her eyes? Well blue mostly, but sometimes looking grey, not black. In form not buxom but yet not skinny.'

There was a burst of laughter, then one man spoke:

'A maid like any other, yet like no other! But such a maid as you seek would not be there. There was a girl kept in one of the caravans of the Gypsies, them with black hair, dark skin and beads and shiny lace all over. They dance and play their tambourines, long cloaks swirling over their skirts. It's good to see and hear them after all this waiting for the next battle.'

'And the girl?' I asked. 'Did she come out?'

'All we saw was a face, a pale face, fair hair, not like the gypsies, and beads were there none. One of the men wanted her but they drew her back from the window and sent the soldier to other business.'

'It must be Rose,' I cried, 'did you hear a name?'

'Nay, then, but she looked a Rose alright.'

11

That night I slipped away to the field where the baggage trains were waiting. It was a big area and the confusion great. Among the craftsmen were the seamstresses who would restore torn and tattered uniforms and standards. Some of them were stitching in a large open wagon whose floor was littered with coloured cloth. They were laughing and I wondered whether Rose might be among these women. I wondered, too, whether they rendered other service to the soldiers than mending their uniforms. They were eyeing me with curiosity and their talk was rough. Rose would not have endured this, unless kept there against her will.

'Must keep our soldiers in good heart,' a woman was screaming at one of the few men there, whose reply was quick. 'Good heart?' he roared, gesturing to where his heart most surely was not.

There was much laughter as they offered me their services together with the terms of their trade.

''Tis early you come. You'd be cashiered for this. Slip away when it's dark.'

'I've come not for this,' I responded. 'I know thy

trade. I've come for news.'

They were all attention now.

'Military secrets? Since we don't lie with Cavaliers, we don't know their secrets. But old pock face over there would lie with anyone she could get, anyone who'd pay her.'

The woman was indeed, badly pock-marked, and a fight followed with clothes torn and hair pulled. But it stopped as suddenly as it started and they crowded round me again.

'News?' asked one. 'Art thou a Cavalier wanting secrets from our army? Even if we knew we'd tell no King's man. We are good for Parliament.'

'Only good enough to put up your price!' I snapped. 'Ye'd be King's whores soon enough if it was worth your while. To women like you one man's the same as another.'

I looked around me carefully, remembering my mother saying, 'Among the bad there's always someone better than the rest.' There was another group of women, quieter and of better manners who were glad to talk. Their stories tumbled out: left destitute by the war, their menfolk impressed into one of the armies, little news of them, they could be dead. One woman pressed a crumpled, stained piece of paper into my hand. She reminded me of Nan, Nan as she would be ten years hence, Nan if the world had treated her badly and she had not come to the Sedley home.

Her voice was quiet and gentle as she begged me to read it. The news it brought was not new, the date was 1642, and it was obvious it had been folded and unfolded many a time. She had surely heard the words many times, the words telling of the death of her husband. 'He met his Maker valiantly, knowing his cause was good.'

I looked again at the woman with her eyes dull, her hair lank, her mouth drooping, her shoulders hunched forward. Nan in other circumstances. Was The Cause in which her husband died worth it? Was any death worthy of a cause? I felt only sorrow for the women among whom I was searching for Rose. Driven by unhappiness or despair was it possible Rose could be in such company? Was it possible Rose was carrying our child?

A motherly woman, not young but not yet old, came forward and I told her of my search. She knew the camp followers well enough, the maids and mothers, wives and widows, the good and the bad, but no-one of Rose's description.

'But doesn't look only for a maid now?' she asked. 'There's many a maid in the army serving like a man, doing all that a man could do. Look everywhere and anywhere. You'll find your girl as likely as not serving in man's attire. There's many does it, following their man to war. I'd do it too if I still had my man.'

There was laughter as she looked down at her drooping breasts and ample thighs.

As I made to leave, the sound of music and laughter came from nearby and the cry of 'Gypsies' was in the air. I thought of the soldier's story of the pale face at the window of the caravan so I followed the women hoping to find news of Rose. We found them soon enough, dancing and singing in the silks and brocades I knew so well, their heads covered with bright, tinkling beads and tinsel. And there, surely, was Ezekiel himself.

'Hey, my handsome trooper, Hast decided we were right after all? Hast given up thy regiment for the wandering life?'

'Ezekiel, you must help me!' I replied, for my mission was too urgent to jest. 'I'm looking for a maid, perhaps with the army, perhaps in men's uniform. I heard of a fair girl with the gypsies, looking out from a caravan.'

'That girl is safely with her kinsfolk now. There was trouble on her father's farm, some shooting, no one left save the girl. We kept her here with us till we found out where her kinsfolk dwelt and I took her there but today. We see, Anthony, clearer than any other folk, what this war does to all of us in its horror and confusion.'

I noted he was drawing on his old clay pipe again for this was no time to impress with the new silver one. He asked if it was the lightsome girl I was seeking and I told him it was not her, for she was safely with my mother, but Rose Eliot, my cousin. Ezekiel remembered her well, for gypsy memories are strong, but had nothing to offer. Just then a young boy came over. He recognised me and told me he'd seen Rose riding on the London road with two troopers. At first, he'd thought it was three troopers, but he was in a wood later and came upon the three of them. One was clearly a woman, doing up her hair which had come down. He had recognised Rose, the girl he had danced with years before.

'A Romany never forgets a face,' he said proudly.

'Did you not talk to her, ask where she was going, what was her business?' I cried.

'A gypsy and a trooper! That could never be, for how would I explain my own business in the wood?' he laughed.

One of the gypsy women saw my distress and stepped forward.

'There's many goes missing these days. It's the fever

gets into their veins. They have to be up and doing something that maybe their mothers wouldn't approve. I've seen wives and widows and maids tending the wounded, going about it as though 'twere their life's work, disregarding the dirt and the blood and the pain.'

It would be like Rose to turn her talents to nursing. There were hospitals in London where the wounded who were not cared for near the battlefield would be taken. There was talk of providing special military hospitals for the wounded but I doubted if they were ready. That left Bartholomew's, Thomas's, Bridewell and Bethlehem. Bridewell for vagrants, Bethlehem for the insane, the other two were more likely to be caring for wounded soldiers. I knew I must follow Rose to London. It was not difficult at that time to get leave and a Parliament man with a pass from his regiment had little difficulty in entering the capital.

London was much as I remembered it, save for the soldiers, and enquiries soon brought me to St Bartholomew's which, for no special reason, I had decided to try first. I knew it was big, that nursing was only part of its work and that it also housed the destitute, the pauper and the rootless of society that flocked to the capital hoping to find a kinder refuge than the country offered. The old lady at the door was surly and unhelpful, drawing on her blackened pipe with a great sucking sound that sent the spittle cursing down her chin. She would not answer my questions about the girl I was looking for. It was the clink of money in my hand that showed the matter would not rest there. A man, surly and uncouth, stepped forward. Coins changed hands and I was on my way following this porter. We went down evil smelling passages, up rickety, vermin-ridden stairs, while a confusion of sound grew ever louder. I thought I must have come to Bedlam by mistake. We stopped by an open door, and while I choked on the foul air that hung round the portals like a loathsome cloud, I began to distinguish the sounds that came from within: shrieks of pain, groans, imprecations, cries for water, appeals to end the torture, curses on the war, the King, the Generals, the raised voices of nurses as they tried to be heard over the din. When I forced myself to peer within, I made out a long, narrow room with but three or four rows of rough mattresses, seemingly no more than stuffed sacking, many with the straw falling out. Here and there were one or two roughly made beds that raised the mattresses on rickety wooden legs a little above the ground. There were two or three – I saw even four – men on each pallet, with a filthy piece of cloth for covering, while between the mattresses there was barely room for a nurse to pass.

Worse by far was the floor and the stench rising from it. It was made of wood, wet in the worst places, damp in the best, while a mixture of water and organic matter oozed between the boards. The room was airless, every window being tightly shut. As I took a few paces into the room men near me called for help in their pain, or for water, a few were cursing, some openly crying, only a few were sleeping restlessly. I saw a doctor, probing with his finger into a wound in a man's thigh and shut my eyes. All I could see was Robert and Edgehill Field, all I could hear were the screams of pain. Women were doing their best to help the patients, dressing their wounds and washing their shattered bodies but all they got were screams and curses for the pain.

I had seen wounded men on the field of battle. I had seen my own brother die of a gunshot wound. I myself had felt the pain of the sword thrust in my thigh. Yet I was not prepared for this hospital ward. I looked at the women, not one of them was Rose, so I asked if a young woman by the name of Rose Eliot had been that way.

'Why yes,' a girl replied, 'she was here till a few days ago. Friends came for her, a man and a woman.

She'll be back when the fighting starts again, it's quiet at the moment. There was talk of a baby.'

A great fear came over me and my head was swimming with the heat and stench of the room. Rose pregnant after all, how could that be? It was only seven months… I must find her.

I left the scene of desolation and knew not where to go. The name of William Walwyn came to me then. The most powerful man in the city, he who knew everyone and everyone's business. He, if anyone, would have news of Rose. I set my steps to find the merchant's house and was pleased my memory for places did not fail me. Exhausted and unkempt I reached Walwyn's door just as the merchant was leaving the house.

It took him only a moment or two to recognise me. With no ado he took me into the big sitting room and called for food and drink. Just as when I first met the merchant, I had a feeling that Walwyn understood everything, that he was the centre of a web, that he could set events in order when the time came. He was quiet now, watching and waiting for something, I thought. While I ate and drank thankfully, feeling no need to break the stillness of the room, he spoke about the war.

'This fighting did not have to happen. Too many

people acted without understanding, following emotion rather than reason, precent rather than reality. Who really understood the situation? You all fight for different things. If you're for the King you fight for Prerogative, for Order in Church and State. But what kind of order? If you're for Parliament you fight for Liberty, for Freedom, and God knows what you mean by that. Shaking off anything that irks you, doing what you like with no regard to the other man, where's the end of that? And what's this thing we call democracy? Your sectaries, who will give every man a voice in religious affairs will begin to speak of state democracy, that every man should have a voice in affairs of state. Is his judgement ripe for such a responsibility? Look around and ask yourself: should HE be trusted with a voice in government – or HE – or HE? And if your voice prevail this year, shall not the other's prevail the next, or the next, or the next? With such a giddiness in affairs of state who shall win? Or shall we not be losers all, a prey to this man's persuasive voice or that man's desire? Already some men talk of going out on to the common land to sow and reap. And where's the harm? Let poor men reap the common and take the produce. But what if men take the land that's sown by others, the pastures with the sheep, the grazing meadows with the cattle? Shall we ask, 'Is thy need greater than his who had it before?' And shall not one with greater need take it from thee in like fashion?'

Walwyn motioned me to a seat by the fire. It was clear that he would come to my story in his own time and I, in spite of my anxiety, could not hear enough of his words.

'Taxation,' he continued. 'You complain of taxation, speak of 'freedom from taxation.' Those are but words. Neither side can win this war without money. Either you give it freely or you're taxed for it. And how much is given freely? There is not sufficient to clothe one trooper for one year and surely not finance an army. So, there must be taxation that has nothing to do with freedom, only with the desire to win the war. The only freedom that counts, the freedom that is fundamental to all else, is the freedom to speak your mind without let or hindrance, to make war with words on people's minds, not with swords on their bodies. I tell you; the field of physical combat is of no importance compared with the field of ideas. You can defeat the King ninety and nine times and kill him for a tyrant, but unless you win a victory over the minds of men you are defeated still. For my part, all the war I make is to get victory over the understandings of men.'

With this he stood up, shook his head slightly as though to rid himself of some oppression, and bad me tell him my story.

12

Far from being surprised Walwyn took up Rose's story. Yes, she had been nursing at Barts, diligently and well-loved and blessed by the wounded who came within her care. A wounded soldier turned up one day whom Rose recognised, indeed they recognised each other. He chuckled.

'It was none other than my niece Lucy! Her wound was slight but enough to reveal her sex. There was nothing now to separate the girls so Rose went off with Lucy. She had done good work at the hospital and now wished to be nearer the action. Where they went, I do not know. Walk now in Paul's and get the latest talk and then be on your way. Don't worry over the girls! Lucy made a good soldier and I doubt not Rose will do likewise.'

Before I left there was one question I had to ask, but I found it difficult to find the words '…at the hospital, there was talk of a baby…'

'Ah, yes,' said Walwyn, 'that was Elizabeth, pregnant again. Rose assisted at her lying-in before she went off with Lucy.'

A huge cloud lifted and my step lightened,

knowing the talk was not of a baby for Rose and me. I made my way to Paul's where the ruinous condition of the great cathedral saddened me. Ramshackle shops and stalls leaned heavily against the outer walls as if to pull them down, while the loud sound of bargaining drowned any more normal trade that might have been taking place. I had heard of Paul's walk and the talk and news mongering that went on inside the building but was still amazed at the scene that greeted me as I entered. The church was full, not of worshippers or priests or religious observants, but of lawyers in sombre black, men dressed as merchants or shopkeepers, people who looked like Parliament men walking up and down in groups of two or three, even a few soldiers in their regimental colours. News vendors, though not as many as in Westminster Hall, offered their printed sheets while others were scribbling, leaning against the pillars of the long aisle to give them support. So this is where our news comes from, I thought sadly. I myself collected several versions before I had been in the church for five minutes: the King had left Oxford and was marching westward; no, he was too involved in domestic affairs to think of battle; the Queen had brought him no comfort but was setting the Court by the ears; Digby and Prince Rupert were not on speaking terms and had nearly come to blows, it was the King himself who had separated them; my Lord Holland would re-join the Parliament having got the Queen with child; no, not Holland, it was my Lord Jermyn, who had travelled from the continent with the Queen, was her lover; no, she was not pregnant but was ill and hated Oxford.

Feeling I had learned little of import and nothing about Rose, I left Paul's and made my way westward down Fleet Street, past Temple Bar and into the Strand, the route John Lilburne had walked at the cart's tail five years before. I glanced up at the window where Rose and I had stood to witness the cruel procession. As I turned at Charing Cross to enter Whitehall, I found myself caught up in a crowd of angry women making their way towards Westminster crying for 'Bread!' 'Justice!' 'Relief!'

In Palace Yard, where Lilburne had suffered, the crowds of women were thick, all crying for Parliament to accept their petition. Towards the front of the crowd were two young women. I could see little but their heads, but the one was surely Rose with the same brown hair, the same set of the shoulders. And the girl with her was surely Lucy. I began to push my way through the crowd towards them calling out 'Rose! Rose!'

Several women eyed me angrily as they let me through, but a soldier tried to stop me, shouting abuse as he did so. My composure broke at that and in the space cleared by the soldier I managed to draw my sword. There were cries of terror as the girl I had thought was Rose turned round, and I knew from the hard look in her eyes it was not her. The soldier in his turn had drawn but I was quicker and with a lunge at his sword arm sent his weapon crashing to the ground, drawing blood from his hand.

I heard the cry for troops and knew that court martial was the only possible outcome of such a foolhardy escapade. Yet, in despair, I would have taken on the whole company of advancing soldiers but for a voice at my elbow.

'Follow me! Discretion is the better part of valour!'

It was, indeed, the Player King. A protective group seemed to form around me as I was marshalled deliberately and without undue haste from Palace Yard while the soldiers were making their way through the crowd. 'That,' he said, 'was close. You'll need to lie low for a couple of days and then 'twill have been forgot.'

I was taken to a house nearby in Petty France and told 'Bide here till dusk.' An old woman waited on me, brought me food. I heard the cries of a baby and a young woman approached whom I had no difficulty in recognising as Elizabeth Lilburne. We exchanged news. John was with the army in the Eastern Association but was increasingly critical both of the army command and of the Parliament. I told her of my search for Rose. Elizabeth knew something of her story, knew she had been restless at home and had contrived to send a message by one of the soldiers in the neighbourhood begging to be given work of some kind. She knew of the need for nurses and so sent two troopers down to give her safe passage to London. Rose left the hospital to help with the birth of the baby we even then heard crying. It was hard to know which of the regiments she and Lucy had enlisted in.

'But now, young man,' she said with mock severity, 'striking a soldier on duty? That's for court martial. They would shoot you for less! But so much is happening now that back in your regiment no-one will know you as the soldier in Palace Yard. But you must lie low for some days. No, not here, Petty France is already suspect enough. John begins to talk again and he asks for pen and paper. You would compromise each other if you stayed here.'

I could only hang my head and wonder at the mess I had got myself into. We talked then of domestic affairs. I held the baby while Elizabeth prepared food.

It was now late afternoon and I had not eaten since breakfast with Walwyn. I was hungry despite of my worry.

It was dark when the Player King returned, looking serious.

'They're searching for you,' he told me, 'so there's but one way we can travel.' He produced a long cloak with a hood such as ladies of quality wore when they went abroad. 'Carry your hat in your hand under your cloak and don't let your sword make a sound. Now, be quiet and follow me!' I kissed Elizabeth warmly and then I was alone in the street with my friend.

We walked swiftly as I followed my guide northwards through what I imagined were the precincts of the Court. Then up the Strand, reversing the direction I had taken that morning. At Temple Bar we turned into the maze of narrow alleys and tenement buildings that I knew was Alsatia, where writ of neither King nor Parliament would run without the assistance of a posse of soldiers and the people themselves. I knew the place well enough by repute but even so was unprepared for the stench of filth, overcrowding and decay that hung over the narrow streets whose high buildings kept out the light and trapped the noxious air. There were sounds of revelry as we made our way down filthy alleys, joined by shouts and screams, by laughter and the sound of tankards on wood. My companion put a restraining arm on me.

'They're searching for you now. This is the only place. In a couple of days all attention will turn to the new offensive. Since they know not who you are, you can return to your regiment without question.'

As we talked, he led me through a square where the houses stood a little from the thoroughfare, letting some light in from the summer night. Looking up I caught a glimpse of a heaven bright with stars.

'Look how the floor of heaven is thick inlaid with patines of bright gold,' observed my companion. Even in that tense atmosphere my response was quick.

'There's not the smallest orb that thou behold's't but in his motion like an angel sings, still quiring to the bright-eyed cherubins.'

'Not quite right,' said the Player King, 'not 'bright eyed'... But here you'll have opportunity enough to savour Master Shakespeare.'

As he spoke, he was giving what looked like a secret knock on the door of one of the houses. In a moment a wooden hatch in the door slid back cautiously. I could see nothing but an eye surveying us. The owner of the eye seemed satisfied for the hatch was closed and immediately afterwards the sounds of bolts being drawn indicated the opening of the door. It opened just enough to let us through. The room we entered was larger than seemed possible from the outside of the house. At one end two women were preparing food at a long table by a fire whose smoke had some difficulty in escaping up the chimney. The smell of the burning wood, nevertheless, was welcome after the foul smell outside. A few men were seated round the big table in the middle of the room, one or two of them seeming no older than I was. At first, I could not place them. They were not the ruffians I had associated with Alsatia. There was something wild and free about their dress, yet they were not gypsies. Even as the Player King introduced them, I realized who they were.

'My friends the Players. With the theatres closed there's no work for us now and most of us don't wish to join the army, either side has not the right. Other work that keeps us alive is not pleasing to Authority so we eke out our existence here. And this young man fights for Parliament though he abhors their action in closing the theatres. He's a lover of Shakespeare and a friend of John Lilburne, for whom he's been a help more than once.'

They made me welcome and I thought I recognised some of the actors. My business and my present troubles were then explained. There was no information of Rose but I was advised to try 'Tully's gang' who travelled more widely than this group of players.

The company was pleasing as was the actors' talk. Again, my spirit rose in protest against the Parliament who, by closing the theatres, had condemned men like these to a life among the worst criminals of London. I wondered why they didn't join the King but they were too aware of the injustice on both sides to fight for either. As we talked men came in, sometimes alone and sometimes in pairs. I did not ask but could guess and pick up from scraps of conversation that their need had driven them to petty theft, assuring themselves that they only took from those whose pockets were well-lined. It seemed they had a common purse under the charge of one of their number called Falstaff. He was a large, rosy-faced man who, padded and made-up would, physically at least, do justice to the role.

I came to understand that the Players lived undetected in Whitefriars with a curious understanding with the other inhabitants. They paid their rent and dues handsomely and on time and there were certain services which, in their profession, they were able to offer. They would, most tellingly, mimic the voice of the commander of the guard, calling his men off the chase. Or they would counterfeit the footsteps and the very voice of a fugitive from justice and so attract the officers of the law while the real culprit disappeared. Their contacts over the country were widespread and they could pass on to those tired of the confinements of Alsatia information of zones of safety and refuge where few questions would be asked.

For their part, the Players suffered their confined and squalid lodging to keep free of the civil war and the impressment which was becoming ever more difficult to avoid. As I listened to their talk, I gathered it was not only 'a plague on both your houses' but a deep and growing dissatisfaction with the Parliament who were now proving as intolerant as the King had been. The name of Lilburne came up in their talk.

They were frank enough when it came to discussing Rose. Yes, they had met a number of girls serving as soldiers in the army and one Player recounted the story of an ensign, commended by his officer, who never shirked duty in or out of battle until the necessity of calling a midwife revealed all.

I froze. Could that be Rose? Had she been pregnant after all? Or was it indeed Rose but some other father, and she light-moralled after all? The words would not leave me, 'Get thee gone for a wanton.' But talk was of a north-country ensign whose speech would make you laugh and who followed her husband to the wars knowing she was pregnant.

No-one came to search for me, they being all too busy. There was much talk, it was reported, of the armies training in the Eastern counties under a squire named Oliver Cromwell. 'What match can a country squire and his tenants, armed with pitchforks most like, be for the King and his Cavaliers?' they asked, and I joined in the laughter. I remembered that laughter in the years to come.

On the third day they considered it safe for me to leave. I was no closer to finding Rose but needs must I return to my unit. As I prepared to go one of the players came in laughing. He said something to the Player King who straight way called.

' Anthony! It's so simple. What fools we have been. Come! Keep your cloak around you. Follow me!'

Wondering, impatient to be off, I bad farewell to the Players who had so courteously received me. I swore I would be there to watch when they took up their craft again. But, I thought to myself, unless the King come back speedily these boys who now play Ophelia and Desdemona will be Falstaff and King Hal. And the present Falstaff? Taking money at the door if he'd still got his wits about him!

The Player King was calling. I was confused by the twists and turns through narrow alleys and up and down rickety stairs that at last brought us out to a desolate riverside landscape where a few huts were the only signs of life or habitation. The air was dank and putrid, the masts of ships showed where the river lay. The Player King picked his way carefully to a building rather larger than the rest. There was something of the farmhouse about the place, yet all was so run-down and derelict that it was impossible to make out anything but broken stones which might have formed part of a pig sty. There was a tether for two horses amidst the waste, the windows were boarded up and the door seemed securely fastened. The Player King gave a signal that caused the door to open to what was a comfortably furnished room lit by windows at the back of the house. At first, I knew not what the clanking sound was which came from overhead, but when I mounted the narrow stairs, I saw two machines which, even in my ignorance, I knew were surely printing presses. Tending the presses, feeding paper into them, folding the sheets, cutting them, stitching them together in pamphlet form were several people. An older man, introduced as William Larner, was directing the others. Operating the presses was a fine-looking man of strong physique with red hair called Thomas Johnston. A beautiful young woman with auburn hair reaching down to her waist, casually tied at the nape of her neck, was moving from one machine to the other and seemed to be checking the printed sheets from a manuscript in her hand. She took the sheets then to a girl who was seated at a table and appeared to be checking the page numbers. Finally, in a far corner, a boy and a girl were stitching the sheets into pamphlet form. The woman who was checking the printing was introduced as Mary Overton, the wife of Richard Overton whose name of Martin Marpriest was known to many for his beliefs in the equality of all men under natural law and his demands for the abolition of mandatory tithes and the return of enclosed lands to the common use. I was so intent on looking at her famed beauty that it was some time before I came to observe the girl stitching in the corner. When she turned and looked up from her task, I saw it was Rose! Rose with her hair after the style of Mary Overton, loosely tied at the nape of her neck and falling down her back. Not the glowing auburn hair and pale face of Mary but the beautiful, lustrous brown hair and pink cheeks I remembered– 'Go, lovely Rose'…

'Rose!' I was on my knees before her, my arms around her waist. She said nothing and I could only murmur, 'I've been searching for you Rose, searching everywhere. Why did you go away without telling anyone?'

Before any reply could bring me ease the boy who had been acting as look-out came running in gasping, 'Stationers.'

It was clear there was a plan for such as this as printed sheets and manuscripts were quickly gathered while the men struggled to conceal the presses behind a false partition which they pulled out from the wall on either side. The boy flung a rope, well secured to the floor, out of the back window, down which the women descended. The banging on the door grew louder as the Player King opened the door with mock indignation.

'Zounds! What's amiss?' he cried. He had pulled his garments as though he had just risen from bed and I was quick to follow. The Stationers darted upstairs, coming down with Johnston and twisting his arms so that I winced.

'Ask my masters then,' gasped Johnston. 'I brought them here to have their will on the wenches… They be back in the city with their good men now. A prentice boy conducted them here and the same boy has taken them back.'

'Zounds!' swore the officer, 'the apprentice serves

his master well when he brings his wife to the whorehouse!'

The Player King and I were straightening our clothes, preserving still our sullen mien. One of the officers hit me sharply round the head. My hand flew automatically to where my sword would have been, but I barely needed the flicker in the Player King's eye to pretend humiliation.

'Not in uniform either of you? You'd do better fighting the King than cuckolding the wives of honest London citizens!'

So saying he turned. The two officers then mounted the horses which with difficulty they extracted from the soft mire on which they stood, and were away. Johnston was the first to speak.

'Not even the rope ladder! They've even left us that! And the press is safe for another time. Larner and the girls will be safe inside the city walls by now and once there no-one will catch Will Larner! Come!'

He poured drinks from the flagon which served a good purpose. It was sometime later that I asked after Rose. She was living with the Overtons, helping with the printing and distribution of unlicensed pamphlets. I understood the importance of printing to the group who, under John Lilburne's guidance, were building up a party to oppose intolerance and persecution in the Parliament as they had opposed it in the King. That the task was hazardous I did not doubt, and I thought of Rose and Mary and the other girl climbing down the rope ladder and hurrying as best they might through dirt and mire to the city gates. I thought of them falling, injured perhaps, caught and arrested, imprisoned by the Stationers, brought to trial and sentenced, perhaps to Bridewell, which I had heard was a hell upon earth to decent women. But for the time being I was satisfied to know that Rose was safe. The greater urgency was now to make my way out of London without being arrested and to return to my regiment.

Later that day, as night was falling, I was once more in my buff troopers' uniform with Salvatrice beneath me, good and strong after her rest. I began to think of Banbury.

13

But first my task was with the army. I moved about the country with my regiment, listening rather than talking. Listening to the talk between men, listening in the villages we passed through, in the farms and houses where we quartered, listening to the soldiers as they talked round the camp fire at night. There was a growing bitterness in the talk.

Among the soldiers there was the desultory talk of home and family, wondering if the wife was managing the business, whether the farm prospered. Much talk was of the children.

'… they grow fast.'

'… would hardly know them.'

'… they're less likely to know US.'

'… treat us like strangers…'

Then the sad little talk of separation began to take a sharper note. The women couldn't manage the farms alone, not when the horses were taken too. Small businesses failed without the master's hand. There were hardships and often iniquities of free quarter. There was angry talk too of religious freedom. These men were for the most part men of a simple faith, desiring only to be left quietly to their own independent worship which for them had taken the place of the church of Charles and Archbishop Laud. But their leaders, with little freedom for tender consciences, were insisting on a form of worship as rigid as that they had fought to throw off.

As we marched, I was sometimes able to gather news of my father who was serving under Cromwell in the Eastern Association. After the death of Robert at Edgehill John Sedley had been like a man possessed. When he heard of the growing power of Cromwell he rode off with his horse and his weapons to join him. He was a man fighting for a cause he believed in, with a personal grief to spur him on. He became one of Cromwell's Ironsides, of whom it was said that they went into battle with a sword in one hand and a Bible in the other. When my mother heard these stories of her husband, she would purse her lips and say: 'Aye, that's him! The war's brought out his true self. He never was a tradesman at heart!'

But when I thought of my father, I wasn't so sure. Maybe it was the Bible in one hand and the account book in the other. It was the war that had impressed this other thing, the sword, upon him. After the war it would be back to the ledger, but always the Bible in the other hand. And then I would wonder: which accords better with the Bible, the sword or the ledger? The smiting of the Malakites 'hip and thigh' showed there was acceptance in scripture for the sword. And was there of the ledger, for the careful adding of penny to penny, for beating the other man down? I thought of the praise given by Jesus to the man who caused his talents to multiply.

For what was my father fighting? For what had he abandoned family and business of which he was so proud? Fighting perhaps for greater profit, for fewer taxes surely meant greater profit. It was not the poor who had felt the brunt of taxation, for they had nothing to tax, but men of substance like my father and even more like John Hampden and Lord Saye and Sele. Did men really kill each other for these things? Or was my father fighting against persecution? Sir John Eliot had died in the Tower where the King had committed him. Archbishop Laud was imprisoned in the Tower where the Parliament had committed him too and they cut off his head on Tower Hill. The beheading of the poor old man gave me no more feeling that right had triumphed than did the death of Eliot, now become a martyr.

Not until campaigning died down and the armies took up winter quarters did I have the opportunity of riding home. In the winter of 1643/1644, I was often there, noting with pride the resilience of a little community whose customary supports had gone. A few sheep grazed on the hills where Rose and I had rounded up stray animals in the old days, a little spun yarn came into the weavers' looms, a bale or two of simple cloth, nothing elaborate as before, was stored in the big barn of the Sedley home. And once again William Digges would sit at his ledger taking far longer than was needful to enter a scant transaction or two. I saw the bales of cloth lying in the barn unwanted, forlorn; nothing, I reflected, but the strong cloth suitable for army uniforms would be in demand now.

My mother with Nan and Nick lived more to themselves than ever, though still supported by a few retainers. I felt the harmony between them and it brought me closer to Nan. There seemed, indeed, to be a comradeship between us that had been missing before.

On one occasion, having ridden with Nan across the common with provisions for the weavers we heard a commotion from the village green and found the same scene I had witnessed years before with my father. The women were shouting that their cows would not calve, that geese had deserted their nests, that a beast had drowned in a ditch where there was no water, a sow went berserk, a farrow of pigs died.

The children were screaming of imps and familiars and devils, while several of the young women were attempting to tie Sarah Trollope into the position I had seen before.

'Shame on you all!' I heard myself crying as I rode angrily among them, just as my father had done. Most of them yielded as they had before, sullen and resentful, no one spoke. But a boy who had been helping to tie up the old lady turned again to his task, while I in my fury struck out with my riding whip causing a howl of pain. As he dropped the cord he was using, the stories poured out. Sarah Trollope walked through the pastures where the cows were grazing and two of them died. She was muttering curses as she went. The hens were laying no more, the rats were multiplying.

'No, no,' cried Nan, running forward. 'She was talking to me. I was sitting by the big oak tree and you'd not see me from the other side.'

They stopped then; their attention diverted to Nan. In the utter stillness that followed I was aware of the western sun casting a warm glow over the scene, of the pinched, angry faces turned to Nan. She stood facing them with her hand on her horse's bridle while the boy, with his hands to his mouth, attempted to still the pain of the whip. Sarah herself crouched by the water's edge, the rope hanging loosely from her wrists and falling into a coil at her feet.

But it was only seconds before the murmurs grew.

'The young one… she's learning… always at the old woman's cottage… it's since she's come our luck has changed.'

There was no stopping them then. They left Sarah Trollope and made to seize Nan.

'God's wounds!' I cried, ''tis neither woman nor maid but this war itself that strikes to our very bowels and kills our animals, ruins our crops and turns us into devils, into scurrilous tormentors of poor old women and luckless girls. You – and you – and you,' and I did not hesitate to use my whip on women I had known since childhood, 'Come to our house, speak to my mother. It was she took Nan here into her care when the soldiers came and killed her father and fired her house. My mother helped her as she helps you now with provisions.'

One or two of the women looked sullen still, staring at Nan resentfully, but they hung back as I approached Sarah, took her arm with the rope still hanging from it, and led her towards my horse. I beckoned to the boy who had been one of her chief tormentors to help her mount. He looked at his hands, which were now showing the weals of the whip, and made to protest, but I silenced him. Sarah's limbs were cold and stiff, but we got her mounted. She smiled and thanked me, then turned to the boy.

'Come with me, I've balm to soothe your painful hands.'

The boy looked terrified but I commanded him to go and when Nan asked if she should go too, I gave my blessing.

Some of the women had dispersed, most stood there amazed and uncertain. I told them I was sorry for their hurt but begged them to visit old Sarah for balm to soothe their pain. The smiles broke through soon enough and then we were talking of the old days when Rose and I used to play down in the village and they would sometimes come up to the Sedley house, dodging with awe from my father but easily beguiled by my mother into the kitchen for a bag of sweet treats.

It was getting late and I must now go home. We parted on the only possible note:

'Pray God this war ends soon!'

As we grew closer, I knew more about what to expect of Nan, though I still found it difficult to account for her actions. She would never walk by the Cherwell with me or let me show her the haunts of coot and badger. One day she asked about the girl I used to play with down by her farm and who had been given milk and cake. The question surprised me until I realised that Nan had never seen Rose since those days. Rose had moved away to Oxford before Nan came to the Sedley home. I was surprised too that she should have remembered her. I felt the colour come to my cheeks as I tried to explain her. I had many a time tried to explain Rose to myself, but never to another person, certainly not to another woman. The descriptions I gave when I was looking for her were something different, factual only and external.

I talked of Rose as my cousin, knowing that this was not quite true but hoping Nan would believe there was a mere family connection. I told her they had moved away.

'You used to go to the river with her,' said Nan. 'I saw you. I was there too. Oh yes, I know your Cherwell well enough! I saw you together always. I was alone always. You would have shown it all to her before. I would be only second time round. But I know it all already.'

She shrugged her shoulders with a gesture as though to say, 'What do I care anyway?' It was then I saw it all. Lines I had heard from the Players rushed into my head:

'The venom clamours of a jealous woman poison more deadly than a mad dog's tooth.'

Nan's jealousy of Rose, her refusing to come to the river, were clear to me now. But Nan's defiance quickly changed, and it was that rapid change of mood that I was coming to know so well. She was no longer the jealous young woman but the frivolous little girl as she dragged me by the hand and bade me come and see her secrets. I knew them all, the secrets she showed me, but I tried to hide that from her. As we bent over a hole in the bank where a water-rat had made his home for successive years, she caught the twinkle in my eye. For a second it seemed she would push me away as I pulled her close to me. But she jumped to her feet and we walked back to the house slowly and separately. She refused the arm I made to put about her and thrust her shoulders forward.

Nan accepted me more fully after that and so the next time I came home I told her I loved her. Hers was a simple and gentle avowal, like so many of the things she said and did.

'I love you too, Anthony,' she said.

'More than life itself I love you, Nan,' I gasped, overcome with emotion.

I remember her grave look then as she said, 'I love

you, Anthony, I love you as I love my life.'

Only later did I ponder her reply. At the time it seemed to offer all I could wish for.

14

Shortly after, in the June of 1644, I had something else to think about when I found myself once more preparing for battle near my home, proceeding north up the Cherwell with Waller and his Kentish men. We saw the King himself with the Prince of Wales. I had no difficulty in picking out the thin face with its pointed beard and the very dark, round-faced boy beside him. The orders were, 'Shoot at them!'

'We fight to rid the King of evil counsellors,' I was bold to say. 'We fight not the King but his evil counsellors, so we are told many a time. Why then shoot at him?' There was no time for an answer.

We should have won the battle of Cropredy Bridge. As the King's van on the other side of the river quickened its pace there appeared a gap between van and rear where Waller, by throwing a considerable force over the ford at Flat Mill half a mile to the south of the bridge, focussed his attack. But he was not quick enough. The Royalists, perceiving the danger, were able to close the gap before Waller could strike. In the ensuing battle Waller lost the whole of his train of artillery besides many men slain or wounded. Our unnecessary defeat at Cropredy hurt me the more in being so close to home and the scene of happier times. I was bitter at the failing of my Commander, the man who had destroyed the market cross at Abingdon yet could not even dent the King's army.

When the news came of Rupert's defeat at the mighty battle of Marston Moor, west of York, three days later, something of my pride was restored. It was a sadness to me, nevertheless, that his little dog, Boye, (Nick's devil in disguise) had slipped his leash and lay dead upon the battlefield.

We needed all the cheer we could muster from the Roundhead victory at Marston Moor to carry us over the rest of 1644. Our position just outside Banbury had kept us free from trouble but we knew the townsfolk, many of them our friends from former days, were near starvation. It was a relief when in the summer of that year Parliament turned to besiege Banbury, intent on taking back from the King the garrison town he had seized at the beginning of the war.

It was a long campaign with fortunes swinging first one way and then another before Banbury and its castle were secured once more for Parliament. In the Sedley home we cared for the wounded, Roundhead and Cavalier alike. My mother said when a man was hit it mattered little which side he was on. Nan was a wonderful nurse: grave, gentle and cheerful. This was the time when, at last, Sarah Trollope was recognised for the skilful healer she was. The old lady could restore a shattered limb that doctors had abandoned. Torn flesh responded to her healing salves, fevers to her healing draughts. So much was she respected that the soldiers built on to her cottage a large shed which housed the sick and the wounded and became a little cottage hospital. Even the villagers, who had so often tormented her, forgot their fear and helped by making rough mattresses from sacking and filling them with straw and heather.

Strange as it may seem, those days were among the happiest days I had known since Robert was killed. Even my mother, with a new sense of purpose, responded to the atmosphere of healing as she and Nan tended the sick. Old Sarah was often with us, called in to help on some difficult case.

My duties with the army around Banbury brought me home, though only for short periods, more often than before. Nan and I would sit together in the evening light and I would tell her of my dreams of a quiet, scholarly life.

'Nay, Anthony,' she said, 'there's some of us for

home and family, others for a cloistered life. There's some for love, the love of man and woman. Your cloistered life would not allow it. You're better with your books than with your kissing!'

Half serious, half in jest, she slid my arm from around her and stood square before me. I made to catch her to disprove her point. Like quicksilver she was in the stables and without waiting for saddle or bridle was away while I followed on Salvatrice. I never caught her and when I returned to the house there she was, tending the most recent victim of the fighting, taking no notice of me. There were many times such as this when the thought that she was 'fey', a changeling, came to my mind.

In the course of the fighting round Banbury I became aware of a giant of a man, a Corporal, whose vigour appeared unstoppable whenever I chanced to see him. In a lull in the fighting, I found myself at the side of this man who, apart from the grime of battle, appeared untouched by any exertion. He appeared to recognise me and when he removed his helmet, I saw for the first time the curled moustaches, the sharp blue eyes of Richard Thompson.

When it became apparent that the campaign to retake Banbury and its castle would be a long one, many troops were billeted in the villages and houses roundabout. I therefore found it natural to invite Thompson and some others to the Sedley home. Thompson himself was larger than life and everything he did too. His good humour was infectious while his voice carried out to the far corners of the barns with authority. My mother, with the rest, was beguiled, commanding he be brought wine and viands in advance of the others. I could not help observing Nan who was gazing at him as in a trance. His eyes swept round the kitchen till they met hers and, in a voice more soft than before, he swore.

'God's truth! The maid I held before me at the farm!'

Nan had remembered too, there was no doubt of that. She spoke little but as she attended to the food and the table, she followed Thompson with her eyes and hung upon his words.

It soon became clear that the main Royalist force was re-grouping once more for battle. The siege of Banbury was halted and in the early summer of 1645 the armies were manoeuvring over what was once more familiar ground to me. Scouts brought news that Charles was hunting in Fawsley Park on the Banbury Road, the home of the Knightleys. I was with a group of horse, probing forward, when we came upon a party of cavaliers casually eating supper at the inn at Naseby. My men drew first, but you could not run a man through when he was eating his supper! By the time we all had our wits about us there were cries of recognition, many were local boys on one side or the other. So that's what the war's about, I thought, running my sword through the boy I sat with at school or letting him run his sword through me!

When on the morning of June 14, I found myself on a low ridge among Cromwell's cavalry on the right wing of the Parliamentary army I was looking across broken, somewhat lower ground, to a similar small ridge where the Royalist forces had gathered. It reminded me of Edgehill. Again, there was the splendid sight of regiments drawn up in the colours of their commanders, their banners flying and the King himself riding before them in full armour with drawn sword held aloft. I wondered whether the Parliamentarians looked as imposing to those on the other side. I heard Cromwell's exhortation to the Lord, giving thanks for the victory he knew would be his. Indeed, the Parliamentarians so far outnumbered the Royalists that only accident or complete incompetence could deprive us of victory.

I rode shoulder to shoulder with my father as we plunged into the Royalist left wing. I lost sight of him in the rout of cavaliers that followed, but saw him again as we turned to assist the foot in the centre. My regret, even then, was that I was not on the left wing with Ireton to meet the charge of Prince Rupert. Rupert had turned at Naseby for the main battle was already lost. Unlike Edgehill the Royalists left the field to their opponents, there was no question but that we were the victor.

The carnage was sickening. Four square miles of dead and wounded, thickest on the little hill where the King had been fighting in the midst of his cavalry. This surely must end the war. Apart from the dead we took 5,000 prisoners including the wounded. And we took artillery train, powder, baggage and wagons, including the King's personal coach with his private correspondence, the royal standard, the Queen's colours and the banner of every infantry regiment on the field.

But within a month it was not the famous victory of Naseby but the antics of John Lilburne that were occupying the soldiery. Parliament and army, Lilburne was saying, had failed to secure the freedom and liberties they had been fighting for, and he was writing pamphlet after pamphlet to prove his case. In London the people were flocking after him as after a saviour. When arrested he called upon the Petition of Right and produced Magna Carta, 'My birth right.'

'I have as true a right to all the privileges that do belong to a freeman as the greatest man in England.'

It was no surprise when he was sent to The Tower where he sat with the *Book of Statutes* open before him, telling the people who flocked to see him that he would teach them as good a law as any man in England. He had the engagement of an actor and I could not imagine a better King Hal.

Meantime, as a soldier, I was marching and counter-marching while the King tried to gather together another fighting force. But the day came, as I knew it would, when the familiar figure of the Player King was at my side.

'The time is ripe,' he said.

So I rode off to London and visited the communities where the preacher prayed for John Lilburne and freedom of conscience and I attended the Windmill Tavern and the Whalebone Inn where close committees of the Leveller movement met and planned, drank ale and prayed.

The events of those years are as much part of history as the civil war itself. We organised ourselves to win the peace with as much fervour as we had to win the war. Each troop and company had its own elected agent or agitator, each regiment its own Council of Agitators. The secret printing presses hummed with our manifestoes while John Lilburne in the Tower provided more. I rode from regiment to regiment carrying his latest writings, sometimes reading then aloud to the soldiers gathered round the camp fire, standing to make my voice heard so densely were the rows of soldiers packed. It was then, as I read them aloud, that I was able to savour to the full his words. I came to know whole passages by heart and scarcely needed the light of fire or lantern as evening slipped into dusk and the stars shone out over the camp. How he lambasted the Merchant Adventurers.

'... a company of private men who have engrossed into their hands the sole trade of all woollen commodities... wool is so essential a privilege to all the commons of England that whosoever assumes it to themselves are as culpable of the greatest of punishments whatsoever, as those that are guilty of robbing the free-men of England of their birth right and inheritance.'

Meanwhile Parliament's armies began to gather with renewed determination round Oxford, intent on taking the Royalist capital. Now I had much opportunity for visiting the Eliot farm and hearing what they heard of Rose's work. Margery was proud to know she was working at a printing press.

'We must have news. News is important. And opinions too. Rose prints what the wise ones write. It's important,' she repeated as she caught my smile.

Of course, I agreed with her, swinging her round as I used to swing Rose to show how much bigger and stronger I was than she. I felt strangely joyful. The war was nearly over. Nan would marry me. She had never said so, but I was sure she would. Rose was happy in London. At the same time, I felt close to tears. For what? For whom? Tears for Rose and our lost youth? Even if there had been no Nan and I was going to marry Rose, still our youth would have gone. Could we have re-captured the Cherwell days any more than I had been able to catch them with Nan?

It was clear Fred Eliot was finding times hard. He complained of provisions being ordered by the Royalists for Oxford, by the Parliament for their troops, and whichever side he thought he was supplying they were as likely to be taken by the other. There were dark stories of plague in Oxford. People in the villages wouldn't venture near if it weren't for the need to trade. And soldiers would be likely to carry infection, there was at least one case in the village already. And who they owed taxes to Uncle Fred didn't know. Neither did he know if they were on Royalist ground or Parliament's ground. 'Just a general no-man's land!' he sighed. We talked about the Levellers and Rose's important involvement, but when he said he feared the twins would be fighting in all but six months, all I could murmur was, 'Please God the war will be over by then.'

The boys were excited to tell me that they'd seen the King down by the Oxford Road. It was first light when they heard horsemen approaching from Oxford and hid by the roadside. There were three horsemen. One, who looked like a serving man, took off his hat and loosened his cloak as they passed. Another sat upright on his horse, his hair short and without a beard. His dress was rich, his coat fit loosely to the figure, braided and tagged round the waist. They knew it was the King from the way he pushed ahead of the other two as though he was used to leading.

As Fairfax drew the siege more tightly round Oxford, there was worse in store for the Eliots. The whole village, it seemed, was taken over by troops. Fairfax and his immediate staff were in the Manor House, the Eliot farm was accommodating half-a-dozen troopers and their horses. My concerns for the city, however, were unfounded, for Fairfax himself loved and respected the University of Oxford and his guns did no damage to the ancient buildings and their treasures.

15

I rode home after the surrender of Oxford with a sense of relief and achievement. There seemed not much more to do. The King, who had taken refuge with the Scots, must be brought to terms. This should be easy and the terms would include freedom of religion, of speech and of pen. People would return to their trades and callings, taxes would be lowered, and prosperity would return to the kingdom.

When I reached home, I found my mother at her sewing in the high-backed chair she was accustomed to use. Nick came running in from the yard when he heard me.

'Tell me all about it! Tell me about the siege of Oxford. Was there a fire? Did they burn all Duke Humfrey's books?'

I smiled as I shook my head.

'You wouldn't want them burnt, surely?' asked my mother.

'I just thought what a terrific bonfire they would make, like Guy Fawkes,' he answered cheerfully, 'that would have been a very big one if the gunpowder had exploded.'

My mother looked at him proudly as he ran round the room in the attitude of a fighting man with a gun and a sword.

'Richard Thompson hasn't done much to curb his spirits,' remarked my mother.

It was the first I had heard of Richard Thompson and I thought he must have ridden straight from the siege. But if he was seeking me he could have found me easily enough in the army. My mother looked uncertain as Nick, in great excitement, exclaimed,

'He's after Nan! They're out together now. Down by the Cherwell. She shows him all your secrets, Anthony!'

The wave of jealousy and anger that swept over me was accompanied by disbelief. Whatever Nan did, whatever she felt, she would not give away my secrets to another man! There was little time for any thought for the voices that sounded outside amid laughter were surely those of Nan and Richard Thompson. The door opened and Thompson was there with Nan in his arms. Her arms were round his neck, her feet were bare and her feet and her hair were wet.

'I fell in, and Richard rescued me,' she laughed.

I could do nothing but gasp and when she saw me, she was clearly uncertain whether to run and greet me with the usual kiss. How far my mother felt the awkwardness I did not know but she covered her feelings by busying herself to find dry clothes and shoes for Nan.

It was as well that both of us needed to return to our regiments. Thompson had already overstayed his leave and I had no stomach to stay. There were no private farewells and I regretted that I had to ride with Thompson, though nevertheless I found the man good company. It was well there was no mention of Nan.

I spent the Christmas of 1646 with my family in Banbury. I had not seen Nan for six months and determined that now I must bring matters to a head between us. She was as friendly as ever, but even more elusive. I charged her once for taking Thompson to our secret haunts by the river.

'They were for you and me,' I said.

'Nay, Anthony, they had been for Rose before. What did she feel when you showed them to me?'

'But you said you knew them already,' I countered.

'What if I did! They were yours and hers together before you met me!'

Her reasoning, as always, surprised me. She was quick in her responses too. I tried a different approach.

'Was that the way to behave with another man when you and I are going to marry?'

'Marry you, Anthony!' she fairly gasped. 'I never

said so. Never! Never! We talked not of marriage. I love you and little Nick and your mother and I love my horse.'

I was amazed at her passion and the passion of my reply as I took her roughly by her thin shoulders and shook her.

'But you said you loved me! There is love between a man and woman that is different from love for a horse. Maybe the words are wrong. But when you said you loved me and we kissed it was between man and woman who would be man and wife.'

She was sullen now.

'I never kissed you like I kiss him.'

She caught her breath knowing she had said too much and hung her head, quiet for a while. Then she led me to the fallen tree we had so often sat upon, and drew me beside her. I thought at first she was crying, but no, Nan never cried. Even when she came to our house for the first time, with her family killed and her house in ruins, she did not cry.

'Anthony,' she said quietly, 'you must believe me that I love you as I love myself. I would have married you if Richard had not come. But I cannot help it. I knew it from the moment you brought him to the house. I think I knew it from the moment he held me in front of him when they burned our farm. I love you as I love my life. I love him more than life itself, more than the children I shall bear him, more than I love you, Anthony. I could live without you, without children. I could not live without him.'

There was silence then.

'Will you marry him, Nan?'

'Yes,' she said simply.

I did not ride home for the wedding. If my mother was surprised, she said nothing. There was reason enough for my absence as Leveller activity was rising both in and out of the army. The year 1647 was, indeed, one to remember. For the first time in six years there was no major battle between King and Parliament. Instead, the King was held captive of the army while the army fought the Parliament and the rank and file of the army fought the High Command. But their weapons were words. More than forty pamphlets issued from the Levellers' secret presses during the year and I thought of William Walwyn's words: 'All the war I make is to get victory on the understandings of men.'

In many of these pamphlets you will see much of me. My desires, my frustrations, found their outlet in the great call for justice. Sometimes with another, sometimes on my own, I wrote day after day appealing to the soldiers, to the populace, to Cromwell. How I poured myself into those pamphlets! The words came easily, helping me to forget my own troubles. This was the way to use words, using them to find an exact meaning and also to move men. Perhaps I fulfilled my destiny to be a scholar in a way I had not dreamed of. It was Rose who took my work, had it printed in the secret presses, distributed it. She knew the news-vendors in Westminster Hall; she had contacts among the hawkers of books in the City and Westminster; she was familiar with every clandestine press in London and around the city, and with the men and women who operated them. And everyone among the Levellers, men and women alike, knew Rose. Whenever I went among them it was always 'Rose', no other name only Rose. We met often, helping at the clandestine printers and at Leveller meetings.

I remember one dismal day in January, 1648, when I made my way on foot through the twisting lanes that led down to the marshy riverside at Wapping. Mud was thick, often ankle-deep, while the stench of decaying matter, of the tanners' bark, the brewers' yeast, the effluent of the City was great. There were, in spite of all this, a few market gardens surviving above the decay, the shacks of their owners perched above them. At one of these, the home of a certain

Williams, a meeting was to be held. As I approached Well Yard, I was aware of other cloaked figures making for the same spot.

Inside, in charge of the meeting, was Lilburne who was on bail. And helping him handle and sort his papers was Rose. I walked back with her afterwards and tried to take her arm but she pushed me away. When she spoke, it was of the meeting, she thought we had been betrayed. Rose was right. A Government informer had been there and Lilburne's bail was ended. And so began a new relationship in which Rose was the guide and I accepted all she planned. We visited Lilburne in the Tower and it was her suggestion to act as messengers between him, the Leveller presses and the soldiers of the army.

'Who else can act without suspicion?' she asked.

Little notice was taken of the tired looking soldier and the shabby young woman who visited the Tower. We were able to receive Lilburne's instructions, take his manuscripts to the printer and deliver fresh writing paper.

While Elizabeth joined her husband in the Tower, as much to help him in his work as to be with him, Rose looked after the Lilburne children in Halfe-Moone Alley. Many times we were together there, indeed playing with the children we were closer together than we had been since Nan's arrival at the Sedley home.

'Nan is married,' I said.

'Yes,' was all she replied.

'Do you know Corporal Thompson?'

' Yes, he's one of us,' she said as she moved away.

Some time later we set out together from Halfe-Moone Alley with material for the printer. It was a bright summer day and Rose was wearing a blue cotton dress with her hair tied at the nape of her neck in the fashion she now wore it. The kerchief she raised to put round her head was familiar. A little worn, a little faded, but there was no mistaking it. It was the kerchief I had bought for her birthday and put round her head many years before. I remembered her intake of breath – 'it's lovely!' and half expected her to say so now. But Rose was brisk and matter-of-fact. If she remembered she said nothing.

The walk with Rose reminded me of other expeditions. I made to put my arm through hers in the old way but firmly and without emotion she shook herself free.

We made many such journeys. Sometimes the manuscripts we carried were my own, sometimes written together with others, sometimes Lilburne's work. We were in constant danger of apprehension by the Stationers' Company, but Rose outwitted them and the illegal pamphlets circulated in spite of all they could do. If I sometimes longed for the uncomplicated days of our youth Rose seemed to have no thought but of the task immediately to hand.

16

Among the soldiers my close companion was Will Cherwell, one of the first to win the confidence of his regiment, always ready for a tricky or dangerous task, vehement for freedom of conscience and a staunch spokesman for the poor and underprivileged. We both were elected representatives of our troops and we had the rank and file behind us. As we talked one night about our present task and the possibilities for the future, our talk naturally turned to Banbury and our homes. Will had maintained as close a contact with Sarah Trollope as I had with my family. The war had changed her position for the better. Such had been her success at tending the wounded and nursing the sick that she had become much sought after and respected. The shed which the soldiers had built onto her cottage had won fame beyond Banbury as 'Sarah's Hospital'.

'It's always full,' said Will. 'And with water in the well nearby and the concoctions she makes up from the herbs and plants on the common the house is a real ''pothecary's shop. The villagers bring her bowls and jugs to help her ministrations as well as clean white aprons. This is payment for her services for they can afford naught else.'

It was clear Will was proud of Sarah, clear too that he had something else to say. He cleared his throat and removed his hat before he spoke again.

'Anthony, my father may be a Spaniard of noble birth, as some say, but that's not all good, for who respects Popish blood? Or perhaps my father was a pirate, a highwayman, or simply a vagrant. Sarah is the nearest I'll ever get, and the nearest I want, to a mother. Would any respectable, God-fearing family take me for a son-in-law?'

'First,' I said, 'get the girl's consent and then think of the family. If the girl's not willing you waste your time.'

'Aye, but a man doesn't want to upset a family, not a family he's known and respected all his life nearly. Maybe they know what's best for the girl.'

I smiled then as I understood where his affections lay and could only assure him that Hannah was a strong girl who knew right from wrong and always knew what she wanted. But still Will looked troubled as he spoke.

'There's been no chance to ask her. And now, with the fighting over, she's let her male attire slip and half the regiment is yapping at her heels. I mean to get her away and how do I do that but by marrying her?'

I agreed but remembering the old Hannah I wondered how easy it would be. After two years as a man, she'd enjoy the soldiers, in Will's words 'yapping at her heels'. The Captain had found her work to do helping the Commissariat, so she was still with the regiment, checking stores and inventory. Will pleaded with me to speak with her first. I laughed. Will Cherwell! So assertive in all he did, reduced to timidity by a girl! Then I thought of Nan and my own uncertainty and indecision.

'I'll see her,' I said.

When I made my way to the rear of the regiment in search of Hannah there was less hustle, less activity than when I was seeking Rose. Many soldiers' wives had returned home expecting the regiment to be disbanded. There were fewer farriers, fewer wheelwrights, only a couple of women were stitching a Company colour. No more than a handful hung about with the unmistakeable aspect of the regimental whore. The Commissariat was much reduced and I had little difficulty in making my way to the Proviant Master's tent. I stood at the entrance taking in the scene. There were several officers giving orders while others, of lower rank, with lists in their hands, seemed to be raising questions. In a far corner the only woman present was seated at a table with an officer of lieutenant's rank bending over her. No-one questioned me as I made my way through the room to where my sister was sitting. The lieutenant was pointing out something on the page before her and I noted how, in unseemly manner, he was bending over her and how his hand caressed her hair. At that moment she looked up and saw me. She was still pretty as a picture, I thought. Not beautiful like Mary Overton, not lovely like Rose, nor of elfin charm like Nan, but handsome with her fair hair and blue sparkling eyes. Her years of service in the field had not been kind to her delicate skin.

Now I was there I hardly knew what to say. The lieutenant was looking at me angrily and raised his hand to summon soldiers to escort me out when Hannah, with the little giggle I knew so well, presented me as her brother. She dropped her pen and we were escorted to his private tent nearby. We spoke of Hannah's work as secretary or clerk to the Proviant Master, helping to keep and check the lists of provisions needed, supplied, consumed. Her immediate superior was the lieutenant, a man, I reckoned, in his thirties, not exactly handsome but well set-up. His officer's uniform suited him and he had an air as though he had known the Court in happier days. While I was there his attitude to Hannah was without blame but I could sense the closeness there was between them. He was called away after a while and I knew I must talk about Will. It was, however, Hannah who spoke first.

'How's Will? You must tell him I'm fine.'

'He's worried about you. Are you indeed fine?'

She gave me a strange look and blushed.

'The lieutenant speaks of marriage. He's a widower and has no children. Our father will never consent to my marrying Will because of his parents, or his lack of parentage. And because he's a Leveller.'

'But so am I,' I cried out.

'You, he can do nothing about, but he can prevent another Leveller coming into the family.'

I could feel my anger rising as I replied, 'But hasn't the war ended all this talk of parentage and wealth? We've defeated a King, surely that means we have no respect for degree or rank. The thing is, Hannah, do you love Will Cherwell?'

She thought a moment before confiding.

'When I'm with him I do love him. And when John is with me and tells me I shall be mistress of his big house with command of his fortune it is him I love.'

I took her by the shoulders and looked at her with all the brotherly concern and authority I could summon.

'Choose between man and man. Will Cherwell will not be wanting in occupation and substance. There'll be such a flux in the years to come that anyone with Will's ability and strength of character could not fail to support a wife.'

She smiled at me then and I left her feeling that she would soon be back with Will and there was only the opposition of our father to surmount. Our mother, I was sure, was less affected by the niceties of class and social standing. Besides, Will might be the heir to a Spanish Grandee for whom the Sedleys would be not nearly grand enough! But then there would be the question of religion. Whatever were Will's beliefs now, if his father was known to be a Spaniard and a Papist to boot, there would be no approval of the marriage. But then Will's father might be someone quite different, or his mother might have been a lady of rank who ran off with her coachman. I laughed as I considered the possibilities and I determined to ask among the weavers and old Sarah herself.

Will was consumed with indecision about visiting Hannah in the Commissariat. But before he could make up his mind a rumour was spreading through the army that a girl clerk had run away with a serving officer for whom she was working. With heavy step Will and I made our way to the big tent where Hannah had been balancing the accounts. There was considerable confusion as inside an officer and a couple of clerks were sorting through papers with great concern.

'To run away, fine! But to stop in the middle of a page… Do we have biscuit and cheese for a day or a week or a month? Do we have victuals enough or do we procure more? Lieutenant Ingram was due for leave alright and the girl, who knew her job well enough, has gone too. She'll be cashiered for this.'

I was flicking over the pages of the ledger as I spoke and my eye fell on a crumpled piece of paper in Hannah's handwriting. I kept the page open a fraction of a second longer than was necessary so that Will, who was standing by my shoulder, could read the note. Then, as two officers of the Commissariat came hurrying in, I handed the ledger over. In the general confusion no-one troubled to wonder who we were or why we were there, and we slipped outside. Will was white as a sheet. He had seen the note and repeated the words 'He presses me hard. I wish you would come again. He seems honourable but sometimes…' There was no more.

We made enquiries about Captain Ingram. A Somerset man, he had leave of absence but nothing was known of his clerk. As we left, we were surrounded by a group of camp followers.

'Captain Ingram and the maid? We could have warned her. But she wasn't the kind to take notice of us. An honourable man? Well, he paid up alright, paid generously. A hard drinker but took his drink well. Nothing wrong with the man except an over-fondness for the fair sex; never spoke much of his wife or family. Told some she was dead but she was alive alright last time I was home. No children though, more's the pity. Children do steady a man. Couldn't have gone home with a wench surely, must have gone to his other place over Bristol way.'

Will and I fell silent. I thought of my search for Rose. Who could help but the gypsies or the Players? Neither had been seen for some time. The gypsies, indeed, might be on Banbury Heath, and nothing would stop Will from riding to Banbury. He returned with no sighting of the gypsies but information from Sarah. She remembered the name of Ingram as the name of a family from Bristol with property in the city and a small house at Keynsham nearby. Neither of us stopped to think at the time how surprising it was that Sarah Trollope should have such knowledge of the Bristol gentry.

Nothing now would stop Will. With Leveller activity rising in the army, we were needed as never before. I agreed to fill in for him in the regiment while he rode westwards towards Keynsham and Bristol.

It was later that I heard the story. Will was proceeding westwards on the road to Keynsham when he heard a woman's cry of distress, a man's voice of command and the noise of soldiers. He came upon a girl with her garments and hair in some disorder. She was imploring the soldiers to take her home or to take her to her brother in the army. An officer was commanding them to bring her back to his house from whither, it appeared, she had escaped. He was assuring them she was a distant relation of his sent to his house for safety after the death of her parents. But because of some weakness of intellect, she failed to understand the situation and was afraid she would be harmed.

The soldiers were perplexed. The girl spoke clearly and sensibly, but the man was an officer and officers should be obeyed. What would have happened Will did not know but he had recognised Hannah at the same moment as she saw him and rushed to him with such force that the soldiers let her pass and she threw herself into Will's arms. Ingram drew his sword and Will did likewise. The soldiers drew back and Hannah took protection behind them. The fight was grim with no quarter expected by either man. Both proved to be good swordsmen. It was Will, with the frenzy of determination to protect Hannah, who at last stood over Lieutenant Ingram, whose sword was buried in the brushwood. A couple of soldiers moved their sword arms as though to come to the officer's assistance, but he halted them, scrambling awkwardly to his feet.

'Let me explain,' he said. 'Perhaps the case is not as black as it seems. True, I took Mistress Sedley with me, suddenly on impulse, the evening I was going on leave. I was afraid she'd return to her family in my absence. She wanted to go, curious as to what an elopement felt like, flattered at the attentions of an older man, liking the sound of my good estate. Her only worry was leaving her ledger entries incomplete.'

There was a sob from Hannah.

'I was frightened. You gave me no time, not even to finish my letter. And you said your wife was dead.'

'That was my sole untruth. Also, my first mistake. My wife and I have been estranged these many years. There were no children. I did have a dream of marrying you, Hannah, and having a family. But once we were here, I realised it could not be. Too many people know my wife still lives and no priest or minister would have sanctified our union. My second mistake was to think I could keep you out of wedlock. I thought my estate might compensate for the lack of a wedding ring. And when you tried to flee my house, I thought to keep you by force, hoping you might consent to love me.'

As he talked Will let him regain his feet and one of the men fetched his sword which, with a sigh, he replaced in its scabbard.

'And you,' he said, turning to Will, 'are not the lady's brother who visited us lately? Maybe you have some interest in her. So now we shall return our separate ways to our duties. Except that Mistress Sedley is relieved of her duties as clerk to the Commissariat.'

Will laughed as he told me how the question of marriage slipped out and how they rode back on one horse like a truly betrothed couple.

There was great rejoicing in the Sedley home when Hannah appeared with Will. Will had determined that he would tell my mother that he had asked Hannah to marry him and she had accepted his proposal. Whereupon he rode back to his regiment pausing only at Sarah's cottage to make the same announcement to her.

Sarah, aware of the trouble in the Sedley family that would follow the engagement of Hannah to a soldier of unknown birth, went down one evening to the Sedley home. Hannah was there with her parents and with Nan. John Sedley, though still with the army, was expecting disbandment and letting his thoughts run to business affairs. The unaccustomed visit took them all by surprise no less than the genteel appearance and manners of Sarah Trollope. She had produced from her chest a dress of rich dark brocade, suitable for visiting gentry, allowing my father to remove her cloak and lead her to the chair reserved for visitors, as though she was the one conferring the favour. The Sedleys were much taken aback at Sarah's manner and appearance, which put them at a disadvantage, while Sarah herself was fully in command of the situation.

'Hannah and Will,' she said, 'plan to marry and they have my blessing. Wait till you hear what I have to say.'

Hannah could not repress a giggle to hear her father spoken to thus and she told Will later that he sat there open-mouthed.

'I've never known Will's parents and I've never tried to find out for fear of spoiling the relationship between him and me. You must take him as he is: a King's bastard for ought I know or want to know, or the son of a serving wench. From a Papist family or of Presbyterian stock like yourselves. But what is he himself? Physically all that any family could desire. No weakling stock will issue from his loins. He's of your religion, attending your place of worship, fighting with you against the King. He's never done a dishonest deed or allowed an unworthy thought to cross his mind. He's helped those in greater need than himself, he's never complained at my poor cottage or humble fare. And he's never disowned me, never said a word against me in the blackest of times, never questioned my activities or asked about my past. Now, I'll tell him as I tell you. I was brought up as genteel as you in the younger branch of a titled family near Bristol. That is how I was able to help you find Hannah. I took it as a sign that they were intended for each other and that I should tell my story. I fell in love with a man of whom my parents disapproved and together we came here and built our little house on the edge of the heath. We were happy. But he could not endure the outcast's life and one day he went away. I stayed. But my life has been good, especially since Will came to live with me.

The Sedleys were silent awhile till Hannah moved

over to Sarah and embraced her. John Sedley rose and looked at his wife before saying, 'We shall be glad to welcome Will Cherwell into our family.'

17

For some days after he learned of this outcome Will went about, as one of the soldiers put it, like a great beam of light. But one night the flickering firelight showed once more the puckered brow of a man who was troubled.

'That Thompson,' he said to me, 'who married the girl at your house, he's no good and now he's in trouble again. A great one for trouble. It's in his blood. He'll be cashiered like as not.'

Will told of Thompson's gaming at an Inn, losing money, quarrelling, accusing the landlord of cheating and the landlord's wife and others rounding on him. Thompson said they robbed him, they said he robbed them. At all events fisticuffs and sword-pricks, no more, but too much for a serving soldier.

'Nan? Does Nan know?'

'As like as not.'

My mind moved swiftly. The army needed me but if I rode swiftly…

There was no one at home when I arrived. I sat quietly in the big armchair in the kitchen, loosened the buff leather jerkin that had replaced the coloured coats of Edgehill and wondered if I could kick off my boots. Quiet! I realised how little quiet I had known over the past years. Flinging my hat across the room I put my hand up to my face to feel the lines that strife and worry had left. Five years of war and struggle must surely have left their mark.

When the latch lifted it was not my mother nor Nan who entered but my father with a strangely subdued Nick. The greetings between us were joyful, tender, half tearful. We had not met since Naseby. As we sat and began to talk Nick came closely to my side, gazing with some apprehension at the stern officer sitting in the big chair at the hearth which had remained empty since John Sedley rode away to the wars.

'There's trouble in your regiment,' remarked my father.

'Aye! Trouble all round unless we get our just deserts.'

'Just deserts! Zounds, son! You're not one of THEM!'

What precisely my father meant was not explained then, for in came my mother and Nan, flushed with the pleasure of marketing. My mother came forward to greet me.

'My boy! And just when your father's home too. God be praised I have you both here and Hannah over at Sarah's, and little Nick too.'

I stayed a moment longer in her arms than was needful for I knew she was thinking of Robert, killed at Edgehill. Nan was standing uncertainly and I greeted her with difficulty. There was no embrace between us. It was not till after supper that I had the opportunity of asking her directly to come and talk outside. She had no choice but to accompany me. She still stirred me in the old way, but without pleasure, only bitterness. But now I had to talk of Thompson and I told Nan of the tavern brawl and of Thompson's arrest and detention. Nan was still and cold.

'Aye, I know,' she said 'but I believe in Richard. He's impulsive but he wouldn't hurt a woman and he wouldn't steal. There's many dislike him for his views and spread stories about him. I'm surprised, Anthony, that you could believe such things against him. You round on Richard because of me, but that's not worthy of you. You should stand up for him against his enemies!'

She was beating me with her fists and I did my best to calm her.

'Nan, there's nothing any of us can do. He'll be cashiered by his regiment, but there's so much else afoot I doubt if they'll do more. Does my mother know?'

She shook her head and told me it was the Player King who had brought her the news. There was nothing else to do. If Nan was determined to understand and forgive, I could do nothing. I wondered why I had come. I had thought to comfort her but she needed no comforting.

I took my leave of my father next morning and we talked together for the first time in five years.

'What is this nonsense in the army, son?'

'Not nonsense. The men want their wages for one thing. They're eighteen weeks, some of them forty-three weeks, in arrears. And they claim the right to worship in their own way and won't be bound by any established church, by whatever name it calls itself…'

'I know them,' my father interrupted harshly, 'they're thick in my company but thickest in yours. Sectaries, I call them, Baptists, Anabaptists, Antinomians. They talk of 'liberty of conscience' as though every man might hold, aye and practise too, whatever pleases him. I've seen them in London preaching to tinkers, cobblers, weavers, brewers, chimney sweeps. What a giddiness is this! To do away with graven images is one thing, to open the gates to anything a man cares to call religion is quite another. Aye, and all this giddiness in religion spills over into politics. A man who challenges the religious order will like as not challenge the political order, and the social order too. It was the evil rule, not the kingship we fought against.'

'But the Archbishop? You beheaded him. You tore down his images and smashed the windows of his churches and the Cross itself. You, who say form does not matter, thought enough of form to bring all his altars to the centre of the church, like tables. And then you cut off his head. Is that what your religion meant?'

We rode in silence for a while.

'I understand you, Anthony,' said my father at last, 'It's you, I think, who fails to understand. Your freedom becomes licence. Every man will preach and do as he thinks fit in religion, in politics, with the very fabric of society. No law will be respected, for is not my right to gainsay it as strong as your right to enforce it? I see nothing ahead but chaos if your agitators have their way. Cromwell will oppose you, son. And I'll be with Cromwell. Look, set fire to the brushwood as we do in autumn to clear the ground. But take care to put out the fire before it engulfs the corn and the good grain in the barn. We have destroyed the waste, son. You will destroy the granary unless we stop you.'

Cromwell was of my father's mind. Time and again we thought we had won. But as he had predicted, Cromwell knew when to cry 'Halt'. And our protests broke against Cromwell's will. Yet still we re-formed, made new plans.

It was some time later that Thompson's name came up again when several of us were talking round the fire. I had not seen Nan for nearly twelve months, though my contacts with Thompson were close enough through our Leveller activity. Now the men were talking about him and laughing. He was popular, they respected him, and saw little amiss in the story they were recounting of Thompson and the innkeeper's daughter. Her mother accused him of getting the girl with child and he, not the man to deny it, asked what he could do about it since he was already married. He promised, nevertheless, to see the girl through her confinement before riding off leaving them all in tears and the father swearing he'd have him court martialled.

My first thought was for Nan. In spite of my previous rebuff, I was again riding towards Banbury while negotiations with the King for a lasting peace were taking place in the Isle of Wight. I arrived at the house towards evening when the September sun was giving way to an early autumn chill and my mother and Nick were eating their evening meal in the warm kitchen.

'The war's over!' cried Nick. 'Will the King come back? I'd like him to, or perhaps Cromwell will be King instead, King Cromwell.'

'King Oliver, King Noll,' I chanced, entering into the spirit of the fantasy.

'That's like a fairy tale,' Nick exclaimed. 'King Noll and his merry men.'

'Ah but not so merry,' sighed my mother. 'King Oliver and the Levellers, more like. King Noll and the end of the Levellers or King Noll the Levellers' friend.'

'Certainly not the friend,' I replied. 'He must come to terms with the King first,' I remarked.

'Aye! If terms are possible with one so slippery.'

'Poor King!' interjected Nick

'He was so slippery
No-one could hold him
Down he slipped
Down he tripped
None to uphold him.'

My mother was proud of his verses, made up out of his head and proud when he produced his copy book filled with careful lettering. He selected one:

'My father went to fight the King
My brothers they went too
They didn't want to fight and kill
But what else could they do?
The King imposed his ship-money
His church was very high
We couldn't change the church or state
We had to fight and die.'

There was silence as all our thoughts were of Robert.

It was Nick who told me of Nan. She knew her husband was a great fighter but he thought she was worried. She cried much and spent time enough on her bed. I was wondering how I could go to see Nan without rousing comment, but my mother spoke.

'Go to her Anthony. Take her some soup for she's eaten but nothing these two or three days. The Player King who sometimes calls brought her some message. And then Richard came and left her crying. And so she's been ever since.'

So, Nan knew. Her door was bolted but she heard my voice and flung herself into my arms in a way she had never done before. Yes, the Player King had told her that Richard had been womanizing but she wouldn't believe it until he came himself, 'as though nothing had happened.' He was surprised and affronted when she challenged him to deny the story and asked what else she could expect from a serving soldier? He would see the maid through her confinement and that, to him, seemed to put everything right.

Sobbing, Nan became ever more frantic, clutching me. What could I do but gently guide her down beneath me? I had been starved of female comfort all these years and now in my arms was she who had entranced me ever since she first came to our house. That night, as a thief, I stole her. We lay all night together till the morning light cruelly reminded me that she was Richard Thompson's wife.

I was up and about early and before I left, I was glad to see Nan had taken up the household tasks again. She waved me goodbye, yet as I rode away, I asked myself what manner of man I was. I thought of Rose and the cold grass by the little church.

In the closing weeks of 1648, the King was brought prisoner to Windsor and the army once more entered London and purged the House of Commons of those members who would not support it. Now, at last, we would achieve what we had set out to do six years before. Richard Thompson remained much in evidence, following the army in spite of having been cashiered. He slapped me on the back one day in December in evident good humour.

'Our Nan's with child!' he announced. 'What say you to a Leveller christening? Honest John shall stand godfather and you, Anthony, shall hold the child to Church!'

As his voice resounded through the camp, I was left with only one thought. I must go to Nan.

She was composed, seemingly happy. She treated me not as on the last occasion, but in her usual uncommitted way. As I stumbled, seeking the right words, she smiled. I promised I'd do what she wanted, that my mother would help, that our child must not suffer.

She shook her head in that distant way she had as she faced me.

'Nay Anthony, but I know not. Yours or Richard's…'

I could hear no more, bear no more. Without saying goodbye, I turned straight back without rest or food.

Public and private grief went together at the beginning of 1649. I followed with despair the trial and execution of the King. I saw the same grief and despair in Lilburne's countenance. Like me, he had his personal grief in the death of his two little boys who had died of smallpox within two days of each other. The Leveller leader was emaciated, utterly worn out. The fire was gone, he was cold and bitter. I saw the same face looking at me from my own mirror.

'I feel in a kind of deep muse with myself,' Lilburne wrote to me, 'like an old weather-beaten ship that would fain be in some harbour of ease and rest.' But we neither of us could find ease nor rest. When, after a couple of months living quietly with Elizabeth, Lilburne showed me the manuscript of a new pamphlet *'England's New Chains'*, the very title was enough to renew our determination to carry on. So Rose and I set about the task of unlicenced printing. As we walked the city streets, I looked at Rose. Was she less changed than I? I could read nothing in her face. She looked, indeed, much like the old Rose. But there was no blue kerchief round her head. Instead, her dress was sober grey, somewhat threadbare I noticed, and the kerchief on her head was tattered and worn.

She broke the silence between us.

'I must return to the farm, at least for a while. They need me now. The twins are with the army and with a good spring there'll be much to do. And you remember Robert Lockyer, the little boy who used to stand outside Hannah's window all night? He's one of us now. Maybe he and I… he's in the army still, but after…'

Her voice turned to a whisper leaving me in a state of dismay and incredulity. Robert Lockyer! His family had moved to London just before the war. When had Rose taken up with him? Of course, he was a Leveller. I remembered him well, a tall, fair boy, several years younger than Hannah, somewhat indecisive in manner and speech that Hannah would mock in the days when he was courting her and she was off to meet young Fiennes. But a determined lad who would stand outside the house at night gazing up at Hannah's window.

We said goodbye outside the Lilburne home. Rose kissed me then as we used to kiss after a day's outing together. I started to tell her about Nan. I badly needed her comfort, but she would not give it. I felt she knew already and was leaving me to carry the burden as she had done after our loving by the church.

'Anthony,' she said, 'this war has done more than just destroy men's bodies. I believe it's changed our minds too.'

The idea that Rose had changed hung over me like a shroud. I had always assumed that Rose, unchanged, would be there. The monstrous nature of this assumption struck me now to the full, making me question all my past actions and thoughts. I was glad to be at work on another pamphlet: 'We were before ruled by King, Lords and Commons, now by a General, a Court Martial and House of Commons. We pray you what is the difference?'

Even Lilburne could not have done better! We had the bulk of the army with us now. Without pay or arrears, threatened with disbandment or service in Ireland, the army was seething with discontent. Robert Lockyer seized his regimental colours and with about sixty men of Captain Savage's troop barricaded himself in the Bull in Bishopsgate Street, refusing to move or surrender the colours until their grievances had been met. I saw this man Rose was going to marry in a new light. The old diffidence and hesitancy of speech were gone. Here was a Leveller, an agitator, a pious man and much beloved, strong in his beliefs and actions. But fear at what they had done overtook most of his men so that when Cromwell arrived only fifteen were left in the Bull and it was easy for superior force to seize them. They were court martialled on April 26th and six of them, including Lockyer, were sentenced to death. In the end five were pardoned and only Robert Lockyer was to face the firing squad. We did all we could. Petitions for Lockyer's reprieve came from groups of citizens, from the soldiers, from Lilburne and the Levellers. Rose and I worked frantically without food or rest. Together we took one of the longest petitions ever seen to army headquarters and by insistence got through to Cromwell himself. It was the first time I had spoken to him directly. He looked at Rose with sympathy.

'You would have married him?'

Rose hung her head and murmured assent.

'If I pardon him, will you take him away and pledge him to a quiet life?'

I saw the struggle in Rose's face.

'I could do no more than try,' she said softly at last. 'We should have to speak to him first,' she added boldly.

What happened in that talk I never knew. But later there was Cromwell thumping the table again in his accustomed style swearing he would nip in the bud a fresh mutiny and rid the army of a dangerous Leveller. We heard no word of penitence or supplication from Lockyer. He was taken the next day to St Paul's churchyard. Rose, with his sisters and cousins, was with him. He spoke cheerfully to the firing squad.

'I did not think you had such heathen and barbarous principles in you as to obey your officers in murdering me when I stand up for nothing but what is for your good.'

He refused to have his eyes covered saying that his Cause was so just that he feared not the face of death. Then, speaking out to us all with a smile almost of contentment, he said.

'I pray you, let not this death of mine be a discouragement but rather an encouragement, for never did man die more comfortably than I do.'

Rose was looking at him. Her eyes never left his face as the shots sounded. As he fell, she started forward but the soldiers held her back. There was no sound more except the startled birds flying from the churchyard trees and the deep groan of the onlookers.

All we could do was to bury him like a martyr. It was the biggest Leveller demonstration we had seen. Rose walked with the dead trooper's kindred, I marched with the thousand or so soldiers who paced before the hearse in files of five or six. The coffin itself was draped in black and covered with sprigs of rosemary for remembrance. In the middle lay the dead trooper's naked sword. Behind came his horse draped in black. Some two or three thousand citizens and others followed. They all wore, besides the black ribbons of mourning, the sea-green colour of the Levellers. The route was thronged with people, the trumpets sounded a soldier's funeral. At the churchyard thousands more waited. Tom Mercury was there. In describing the funeral he wrote; 'Let Cromwell and Fairfax take note that this is not the way to crush the free people of this nation.'

Thus began the fated last scene. Lockyer's funeral is together in my mind with Burford Church. In Salisbury Colonel Scroop's men declared they had not left their trades and callings and sacrificed the prime of their youth to be deprived of their rights by a Council of State instead of a King, and they were joined by many of Commissary General Ireton's men. I rode off to Banbury where Captain Smith and his county troop were joined by most of Colonel Henry Marten's regiment, by men from Captain Reynold's troop and by others. I did not visit my home. Richard Thompson rode to Coventry and Towcester. When he returned to Banbury his followers were wearing papers with the inscription 'For a New Parliament by the Agreement of the People' in their hats. Whether he spoke to Nan I do not know. Harrison's men were out in Aylesbury. In Bristol, even in London itself, the Levellers were on the move. By that time my hurriedly prepared document *'England's Standard Advanced'* had been unanimously agreed by all the troops gathered in

Banbury. Those three groups were to join forces north of Salisbury and then march westward to join the Bristol men.

In conception admirable. But there were too many factors to mitigate against it. There was the failing resolution of men who had been fighting for seven years, their inability to change their relationship of admiration, respect, even affection for Cromwell into opposition, combined with the almost supernatural belief that Cromwell would always win. It had been easier by far against the Cavaliers but not many could screw their courage to the sticking point when Cromwell was the adversary.

Most of the Levellers at Banbury defected after a brief encounter. Only about twenty men, including Will Cherwell, followed me and Thompson as we rode south. But there was further disappointment. The Salisbury contingent was smaller than expected, the number from Aylesbury also. By this time Fairfax and Cromwell himself were on the move from London threatening to cut off further support from Buckinghamshire. When we reached Sunningwell on the Thames, intending to make for Bristol, we numbered no more than twelve hundred men all told with twelve colours. Cromwell sent messages of conciliation but we thought he was merely trying to find our position and learn of our plans. We did, however, accept what we thought was his promise not to attack without further parley.

We reached Burford late on Sunday May 13th. We numbered then some five or six hundred men. Three or four hundred had gone to nearby villages.

Cromwell, we thought, was still some distance away so we put our horses out to grass, laid our weapons by, and prepared for a few hours' sleep in the church. But it was only a few hours later, about midnight, that we heard the sound of pistols cracking as Cromwell surprised us. This unexpected sight, ourselves weaponless, completed our demoralization. There was little opposition. How many escaped? Richard Thompson and a handful with him, less trusting than the rest of us, had tethered their horses nearby. I saw him cutting his way through the enemy, a very Achilles before Troy. But I had no time to seize my sword and so was held back. The recollection is still bitter. He, as the alarm sounded, was the first to arm, the boldest to fling himself against the enemy. I was a sluggish worm by comparison. No wonder Nan… I had to keep my thoughts to other things as I strained to hear the sound of escape.

And so it was that the rest of us, a mere three hundred and fifty or so, were herded into the church where we remained, awaiting Cromwell's will. The widespread, large-scale mutiny we had envisaged had dwindled, frittered away to nothing.

18

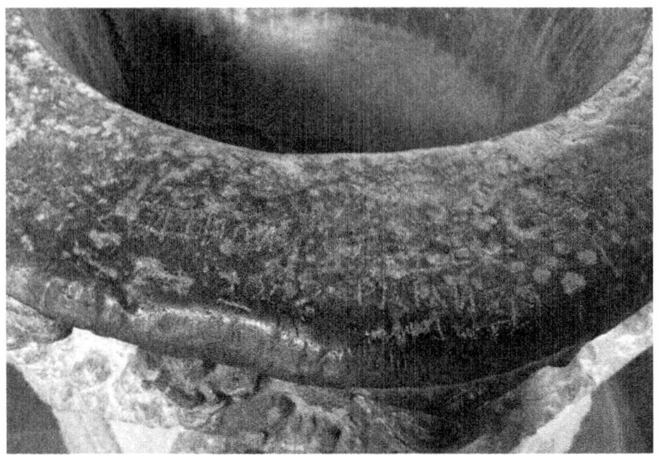

THE ANTHONY SEDLEY SCRATCHING ON THE FONT

I saw the first dawn in Burford Church as, bright and cold, imperceptibly at first, it lit the eastern window. The altar was the first to take the light, receiving shape and colour from the first rays of the sun. What early priest had so ordained the most sacred act of worship, the making one with God, should take place here, where His light first shone? I thought of the words of the Communion, '… the bread we break…' and marvelled that the words should come so easily to one for long accustomed to hellfire and damnation.

The Church was full of the Levellers' sea-green ribbon. The stench of bodies, unwashed for days, hung in the air. More offensive smells began to linger. Men were slouched in the pews, lying sideways or slumped forward on their arms. Others were lying untidily on the floor. A few were sleeping fitfully still. Some, whom sheer fatigue had granted deeper sleep, were waking with a brightness that turned at once to desperation or despair. I watched with pity the return of bitterness, ironed out by sleep, to faces that I knew. Near me I saw young Corporal Perkins, the fair-haired boy, the delicate child, the butt of older, coarser soldiers. What brought him into such an enterprise? The boy sat on the stone base of the font, leaning forward, his head on his arms, a mere child still, with his flaxen hair tousled on his muddy, blood-stained sleeve.

To keep my dark thoughts at bay I turned to the font. In disarming us they had overlooked my dagger and I slowly began to scratch the letters of my name into the surface of the lead that covered the stonework. It cut lightly into the metal. But I got no further than… A n t h o n y… Men were moving about, stamping to restore life to cramped limbs, relieving themselves in a corner of the Church. Some were crouching before the Tanfield tomb. I knew it from visits I had made with Rose, long, long ago it seemed. Now they were calling me.

'Hey, Sedley! You're the scholar…'

I broke the tension briefly by telling them of Sir Lawrence and Lady Tanfield, of their only daughter who married the first Lord Falkland, Lord Deputy of Ireland before Strafford, and of little Lucius Cary their grandchild, the second Lord Falkland who was a poet and scholar, wanting nothing but to pass his life in contemplation and discussion in his manor house at Tew.

'But he joined the King,' murmured someone.

'With inward pain,' I told them, 'a philosopher compelled to make a choice that required action, while he could see too clearly the right and the wrong on both sides.'

'But he fought for the King,' they insisted.

These were practical troopers whose conviction was strongly held without a shadow of doubt and who had followed conviction by action. How could I explain the spiritual torment of men like Lucius Cary?

'He sought his death, they say. Death ends doubt.'

They fell silent then.

'Death ends conviction too,' I thought. 'Will these men be condemned to die?'

I turned back to the font. The careful letters pleased me. But now, before I could continue, raised voices in the Church disturbed me.

'It is their day to-day,' someone was shouting, 'it will be ours tomorrow!'

The commotion in the Church was growing. They were trying to explain how we could so easily have been surprised by Cromwell. Was there treachery?

'Who set the guard last night?'

'Corporal Denne…'

'Our arms laid by…'

'Our horses out to grass…'

'Who said we were safe… ?'

I resumed my work. My hand moved quickly, firmly, guiding the implement that incised the letters… S e d l e y… Later in the afternoon a group of soldiers stopped their wanderings by the font where I was again sitting on the stone step. They admired my handiwork.

'Generations yet to come will speak of Anthony Sedley,' a soldier spoke up.

'But tell 'em why ye're here, lad!' cried an older man.

'Too long a story for stone!' Laughed another. 'Thou't never get it all in, not if you went round and round and round the font from top to bottom!'

They all laughed. They could even laugh! But the older man was insistent.

'Just say thou art a prisoner for justice. Just say the

tyrant Cromwell trapped ye here.'

It was a relief to have something more to do and as the men moved away, I took to my work again… p r i s… I incised. And then the boy Perkins was coming towards me. We spoke of the boy's home and parents. His father had been killed at Marston Moor. His mother, left in charge of their large farm and three young children, of whom he was the oldest, found herself without horses and wagons as well as labourers, taken by first one side and then the other. Her farm labourers had been conscripted to fight; her children were too young to help. She resisted when the tax collector came and her refusal led to physical violence. She was abused and died of shame and shock. He had joined the army as soon as she was buried with no conviction that one side was better than the other but with a burning desire to end the tyranny of the strong over the weak.

I turned back to the font, my mind only half on my carving… n e r…

I continued. When I came to regard the whole and saw the word p..r..i..s..n..e..r I could not help a wry smile. Well, it was clear what was meant. I couldn't alter it now. The desperate tiredness of days of marching with little food or drink was upon me. My thoughts went increasingly to food. No-one had eaten since our imprisonment the night before, and even then, our bellies were but lightly filled. The regulation pound of biscuit and half a pound of cheese would have been a feast. We waited all day. Towards evening there was a movement outside the church, the big south door was opened and two armed troopers stood guard while two more brought biscuit and ale. The prisoners nearest the door helped in its distribution. It was a strangely ordered, even a domestic scene. Some faces showed resentment, a few men displayed anger, almost snatching at the food. For the most part they were quiet, inward looking still, as though asking why their enterprise had ended here in Burford Church. The meagre meal had put heart into some of the prisoners, whose minds were turning now to possibilities of escape. One or two, like me, had their army knives with them still and spoke of forcing a door or a window. The evening passed with the sound of blades chipping at solid locks. But with knowledge of the court martial sitting beyond the oaken door and the stone walls of their prison, enthusiasm waned.

We all knew Cromwell well enough. We knew his changing moods, the scarcely bridled passions of the man who, acting always as the agent of the Lord, had led us to victory over the King. How would he interpret the Lord's will now? Upon this question hung our fate. Death was the penalty for mutiny. That, no-one would dispute. We had seen it happen. But the will of a merciful God might mitigate the verdict. We looked into each other's eyes and read the same thoughts.

As the Church darkened, the fetid air together with the growing hunger once more induced sleep or reverie. Flickering lights came through the south window as though someone outside had lit a fire. There was the crunch of a boot upon gravel, subdued voices perhaps in conversation, perhaps in consultation upon the prisoners' fate. Occasionally a word of command. I thought I heard Cromwell's voice, that strangely high-pitched, nasal voice that could both command a battle and commune with God. Some of the sleepers around me stirred. One man swore – 'For God's sake!' After which I slept fitfully with the rest.

It was the afternoon of the second day when the soldiers came again. I had been moving round the Church. Some of the men appeared, like me, to be far away in thought from the present. Others were talking, telling stories, a few were singing their old marching songs while some were making games with whatever they had in their pockets or could pick up from the floor. I reached the font as the light from the afternoon sun softened the outline of the stone and faintly coloured the letters of my name. I smiled. As I did so there came the sound of the church door opening and silence descended as three hundred men turned to face the open door and the lights beyond. Three officers stepped into the church, one of them with a paper in his hand. I saw that Cromwell had sent his best officers, Colonels Harrison, Okey and Scroop. Did that presage pardon and a harangue on future good behaviour? But there was no harangue, the words were few. Mutiny in the view of the court martial deserved death. There was no mitigation. The sentence was death for us all.

As the door closed on the sunlight outside, curses and imprecations broke from the men. There was the sound of sobbing.

'No, not all! Cromwell couldn't kill us all.'

'If he thinks it's the Lord's will he'll do it.'

'How will he do it? Who will bury three hundred men and more?'

'Who cares about burial?'

As evening drew on, I was aware that something was passing from hand to hand. When it reached me, I could just make out the words: 'The petition of the heavy-hearted prisoners in Burford Church.'

'God's wounds!' I cried, but immediately gained

reassurance. Only eleven signatures were appended to it and it had come from the far end of the church. I flung the paper at the feet of the two troopers who brought it to me, but then I saw young Perkins watching me and I slowly stooped to pick it up. If the boy wanted to sign, it was not my concern. Perkins took the paper from me, read it slowly and smiled at the two men who brought it before saying:

'I have no heaviness of heart. I thank God I had the chance to show my faith in this enterprise.'

He handed the paper back then sat down beside me on the step of the font. We talked a little of the war that divided families and friends, 'the war without an enemy.' We spoke of the right to vote, of the Soldiers' Councils, the Agreement of the people and of John Lilburne held fast in the Tower on Cromwell's orders.

It was dark now in the church. Corporal Perkins sank his head on his arms and prepared to sleep. I prepared to do likewise when voices at the other end of the church grew louder:

'Who set the guard last night?'

'Denne!' came the chorus.

'Judas Denne, Judas Denne!' shouted someone and the chant sounded through the darkening church.

I shivered. Even in the hot, airless church I

shivered. No-one spoke after that. The silence was bleak as we lay or sat ourselves down for our last night's rest. What do men think about when under sentence of death? If I had been asked a week before I would have said 'Eternity' or 'God.' I ought to have said 'Hell fire and damnation.' I thought of the 'Roaring Boy' in the pulpit at Banbury and the sermon I had heard with Rose at Paul's Cross in London, which had sent us trembling to bed feeling that we were the sinners at whom the preacher was directing his wrath.

Now in the church, under sentence of death, I wondered anew whether I had won remission of hellfire and damnation. If I had done so, was it because I had fought against the King at Edgehill and Naseby? Was it because my party had cut off the King's head? But I had never agreed to that, and the anger still rose in me at the memory of the little figure, a long way off on a cold January morning, saying something I could not hear. Then there was the taking off of his doublet, laying himself down out of sight while some minutes later a severed head was held high to the deep throbbing groan from a thousand throats.

Was it more likely I was damned because I had chosen the wrong side in the war? Was it because of this last, desperate stand against Cromwell? Was it because of Rose or Nan? I gave up the struggle to decide whether or not I was damned. This is why, I thought, people about to die think so much of their beginnings, for there is certainty. After death… what? My thoughts turned once more to the King.

He too, had known he would die on the morrow. He had his chaplain with him and they prayed all night. There was no priest here in Burford Church. Perhaps to be in church was hallowed enough. But who among their executioners would admit the sanctity of a church, they who had made a prison of it? I shrugged away the paradox and saw again another church, heard other voices. We had talked high principles at Putney: 'the poorest he that is in England hath a right to live as the greatest he.' We thought it was the beginning, but we reckoned without Cromwell. It was neither a beginning nor an end. The army seethed with unrest; civilians rallied to our support. But Cromwell, massive and impregnable, held us back, as he did now.

There were too many questions to be answered and I turned once more to the font. It was dark but by the light of the flares outside I managed to incise the numbers of the year. The curves of the '6'and the '9'were difficult, but it was necessary to record the date of my last night on earth. I fumbled for the exact day without remembering, decided it didn't matter and lay down by the font. Most of the men were quiet now. They had faced death many times before, perhaps they hardly believed in it.

'It's this damned hunger!' explained one man, more restless than the others.

When the third day dawned, we expected the soldiers, but no-one came until the sun had passed its zenith and the western window was suffused with light. It was almost with indifference that at last we heard the clatter outside, the words of command. We were hungry, drowsy in the oppressive air, without hope. I again felt curiosity to know how they would do it. More than three hundred, the carnage of a battle. Where would they do it? Down in the meadow? But then we could escape, and I felt briefly the cool water on my body as I plunged into the stream to avoid the firing squad. A few at a time? What would the townsfolk of Burford think of such carnage? Cromwell could not do it, not to men who had fought with him at Naseby. He loved his troopers. Fairfax would not do it; he would not have harmed the King.

But the trooper at the door was saying something. He held a soldier's helmet in his hand and there were gasps round the church. But what was he saying? We were to draw lots, the lot to fall on four. Cromwell would take four to prove his might, dismiss the rest to show his magnanimity. Three soldiers made their way to the back of the church with the helmet.

'Here, take!' they commanded over and over again. I tried to make out the progress of the draw as the officer with his two attendants pushed his way round the church.

'All must draw,' he kept saying.

But no man, as far as I could see, shirked the issue. There was no cringing, no attempt to hide. They were standing now in rows so that the officer could better perform his task. Near the end I stood with young Perkins, still by the font. Each of us took a folded slip.

'Wait!' came the command. 'Wait till all have drawn.' The soldiers were vigilant, their guns ready.

'Open!' came the command.

There was a pause, a faint rustling of paper, a low cry, a deep inhalation of breath. Someone laughed, in defiance or relief? Somewhere the cry came 'Denne, Cornet Denne.' He slowly raised his paper with the mark upon it. Then the others, Private Church, Cornet Thompson. 'No, no!' was my impulsive cry as my thoughts raced on and my attention was directed to the boy at my side about to raise the paper with the fatal mark upon it. Instinctively I tried to take it and substitute my own, but the officer was too quick.

'The lot stands,' he said.

The evening was spent in prayer, the four men about to die praying together by the font. They talked of Freeborn John and his message. Would he be next to die?

'He was right,' someone was saying. 'Justice was on our side. But what is justice if someone else holds the reins?'

'With Old Noll in the saddle,' growled a trooper, 'we were doomed from the beginning. But it was worth a try!' he added jauntily, attempting to lighten the tension, though ending on a sob. His brother was one of the condemned.

'Aye! We fought and lost,' said someone, 'not even a chance to fight…' and their wandering eyes fell on Cornet Denne. But if he had, indeed, betrayed them would the lot have been allowed to fall on him?

The condemned men left messages for their families. Someone spoke of following in the line of martyrs like Richard Arnold, shot at Ware, and young Lockyer, shot in Paul's churchyard. Quiet fell. The church was darkening now as the spring sun slanted away from the west window. I watched young Perkins sitting again on the steps of the font, leaning against it, his eyes closed, his lips moving as if in prayer.

'I'm rehearsing what I'll say tomorrow,' he said. 'I pray that Cromwell give us time to speak before they fire. I'd like them all to know I died bravely, upholding our Cause to the end.'

'And so they shall,' I cried. 'The world shall know and generations after shall praise and honour the name of Corporal Perkins!'

I took the boy's hand, forcing myself to be calm.

'Sleep now,' I said, 'shall we pray a little first?'

'Just pray quietly,' said the boy, 'not like Cromwell's chaplains.' And we both smiled a little.

My resolve to stay with the boy till the end was frustrated when at dawn the church doors were opened wide and for the first time in five days, we saw the world outside. The rush of morning air was cold and sweet. The four convicted men were made to stand aside. The rest of us were herded up the belfry stairs. We filed slowly, shuffling and with heads down, guards before and after, and so out on to the leads of the church roof. How unreal it was to gaze out over the quiet landscape at the gentle Windrush, sister to the Cherwell, the meadows thick with kingcups, the drooping willows and the narrow roads leading north and west. Along which one had Richard Thompson ridden in his flight from Burford? Had he gone to Nan? And was Will Churchill with him? But now, mindful of my promise to the boy, I pushed forward to the edge of the roof. There was little resistance. Few had a stomach for the sight we were about to witness. I had nothing to write with but my memory did not fail me. I would never forget.

We were facing the westward churchyard wall. To my left I made out Cromwell standing with a group of officers. He looked dejected, not triumphant. As I watched, someone brought out a table and a chair. Cromwell sat, looking towards a group of men whom I made out to be the executioners, a musket firing party standing at the ready. They took their places facing a section of the churchyard wall. I leaned forward trying to see the church door whence the prisoners would come but all I could see were the tombstones in the churchyard. There was movement away to the left and a group of soldiers escorted Cornet Thompson, Richard's brother. They took him to the wall and turned away. The lonely figure looked round wildly. As I strained to hear he muttered something of the legality of his engagement, of a just God. It was as though he was appealing to his captors, but to no avail. As the shots rang out and the musket balls tore through his flesh the frightened birds swooped upwards from the churchyard trees as they had done for Bobby Lockyer.

Corporal Perkins was the next. He walked forward, his head high, and leaned against the churchyard wall as though posing for his portrait.

'As if,' I thought, composing the words in my mind, 'the sight of his executioners was so far from altering his countenance or daunting his spirit that he seemed to smile upon both and account it a great mercy that he was to die for this quarrel.'

His hair was tousled still and the flaxen locks blew in the breeze like a pennant against the churchyard wall. He looked up and I made a sign. Surely there was a smile upon his lips. He looked then straight up to heaven, set his back more firmly against the wall and bade his executioners shoot. He made no speech but his actions were more eloquent than words.

John Church was the next.

'Supported in his great agony, as in life itself, by his religion.' I recorded to myself. For he, like the other, said no word but pulled off his doublet, stretched out his arms and bad the soldiers shoot, looking them full in the face without fear or terror.

When Cornet Denne was brought out there was a movement on the roof, an intake of breath. The prisoner's head was down. When he looked up it was towards Cromwell. He looked penitent and seemed to be pleading. I made out some of the words: 'I am more worthy of death than life…' There was a brief word of command as he was led back to the church and the firing party relaxed. There were those on the roof who would have thrown themselves down on him as 'Traitor…Judas' sounded from the roof.

Cromwell was now on his feet and looking up at us. I saw him clearly for the first time that day. The tears were streaming down his cheeks and he looked as though he might burst into prayer. Instead, he turned to his officers, shaking with rage and thumped the table with his fist. His voice carried up to the roof loud and clear:

'This is all Lilburne's doing!' he was shouting. 'Lilburne and his seditious scribbling. I tell you gentlemen, either he or I must perish for it!'

Shortly afterwards we were escorted down to the church, more foul smelling than ever after the sweet air outside. Before we were released, we had to listen to Cornet Denne preach repentance, followed by Cromwell himself. He mounted the pulpit to tell us how the Lord had spoken and managed affairs in his own way. We listened to both men in silence. After that events moved quickly. An officer by the church door was handing out passes.

'Passes under His Excellency's hand to take you to your homes. Find your mounts if you can. Instant death to any not dispersed by nightfall.'

They almost stampeded then to get away before there could be any change of mind. Many, in particular the men of Oxfordshire, walked or ran away not waiting for the dim chance of finding their horse. They were all gulping down great draughts of morning air. One man was sick as he grasped his pass. 'Dirty swine!' exclaimed the officer whose coat was fouled. But the man had gone.

The spring sun was climbing high. I thought of Salvatrice, not an easy mount for another rider. Maybe she was still there where I had grazed her on that fateful night. Great was my happiness when she bounded towards me. I wanted to stay a while to see where they would bury my comrades but the cry of 'Out! Out! Or it will be your turn!' deterred me.

So, each man rode away, each to himself, no joy of unity, no strength of common purpose, only the backwards glance to the churchyard wall and the Cotswold earth where the Levelled men would find their rest.

19

My thoughts quickly turned to the need to find the Mercury man. I must find him and record the shooting of the Levellers in the churchyard. As I rode, I remembered the last words of Corporal Church and the story I would write of Corporal Perkins. Thus occupied I failed to see the oncoming rider until we were almost abreast and the other was drawing rein.

'Anthony Sedley, by all that's holy! In God's name where has't been? Are t'others still in church in Burford?'

'Tom Mercury,' I cried, 'In God's name take this down.'

And to the bemused news writer I began to pour out the words, stumbling over them like a drunken man, reeling in the saddle. We turned our horses then and made for an alehouse less than a mile away. There at last, unkempt, unwashed, unshaven and haggard, I tasted food and told my story. My thoughts were racing.

'Richard Thompson? Has't news of Thompson?' The words '… and Nan?' stuck in my throat.

Tom's face was grim.

'Corporal Thompson put up a gallant fight in Wellingborough wood…'

'Yes?'

'The odds were great. He dealt with all before him but they sent one behind. Shot him in the back…'

'And he…?'

'… is dead.'

Richard Thompson dead? More than Cromwell's victory this spelt the end. Thompson was more real than Lilburne. Lilburne was in the Tower, Thompson was with us. But underneath some other consideration was rising, barely recognised, unacknowledged. Nan! Nan, great with child, his child or my child. I saw myself breaking the news of Thompson's death to her. How I would take the child, be a father to it for Richard's sake, for my own sake, for her sake. And would she then be glad to take me as she so nearly had before Richard came? And Nan and I would have more children, and they would tell the story. I would never grudge the admiration due to Richard.

The Mercury Man was looking at me strangely.

'Here, lad, another drink…'

I knew I must ask the question, but there was no need. The news writer was speaking again.

'Mistress Thompson hath the news… great with

child… near her time… fell into labour when she heard… and she and the child are dead.'

Many hours later I found myself by Port Meadow on the Thames above Oxford. I remember nothing of the departure of Tom Mercury, nor how I turned my horse away from Banbury, skirting Witney and crossing by Hanborough Bridge as King Charles had done when he rode from Oxford with his army six years before.

In sight of Oxford my thoughts went to the defeated King. Of what was Charles thinking as he rode from the city? The coming campaign? Or was he thinking of his wife, that sparkling little lady who had patted Rose on the head? Or of his children, all younger than I was? He never saw his wife again. The tears ran down my cheeks, but whether for the King or for myself I did not consider. Those words I had heard from the Player King all those years ago were indeed prophetic:

'Oh War! Thou son of hell.'

I turned again then, skirting the rise of Shotover. I rode round the city's rim then took the well-known bridle way down through the sloping fields, mellow with half-grown corn, past the church and the burnt-out ruins of the Bishops' Palace at Cuddesdon, down to the cottages of Denton nestled by the brook. I turned upwards through the much-loved lane I knew so well, now flanked with cow parsley on either side. I was hesitant to face whatever reality I might find. On the high ground by the little church where Rose and I had come together I looked across to the clumps above Wittenham, still standing out thick and green, untouched by war. I rode slowly down the flagged path by the cornfield, trodden by countless generations. Salvatrice turned without hesitation into the big farm gate and halted by the tether I had always used.

I heard Rose's voice about some simple task outside the house and I stood where I was until she saw me. Slowly she came and led me in. Margery was there, busied about the evening meal, while Old Ben sat in the chimney corner, tankard in hand.

Tiredness, like a shroud, enveloped me. No need to think. Something was over, finished. When you finished you could rest, whether you won or lost you could rest. Strive with all your endeavour then rest. Death was rest. They rested in the churchyard by the churchyard wall. Three shots, one after the other. Why not all together? How soon did they find rest? The command, the shot, the musket ball flying too quick for the eye to see. I did not see the moment they entered the living flesh. Was that the moment Corporal Perkins found his rest? And Thompson? Did they bury him in Wellingborough wood? And Nan and the child, perhaps my child, I hoped they were buried on the wild heathland where surely Nan had her being.

I opened my eyes. Margery was busy at the hob.

'Hot soup?' she asked.

My story ends in 1660. Lilburne was dead. Cromwell was dead and the government he had established perished with him. Not the son of Cromwell but the son of Charles I held the reins of power. Neither Cromwell's army nor Lilburne's Levellers but another Stuart King had been welcomed by a country tired of strife. Passion and heroism lay dormant and the heroes and martyrs of the many-sided struggle were remembered by only a few. I took those few to Burford church on the day the new King entered London. I had never thought to go back. The three of us stood by the font. The boy eagerly traced with his finger the letters he saw there.

'A n t h o n y S e d l e y,' he exclaimed. 'My name!'

We wandered round the church for a while but the boy was impatient to go outside.

'Is that the wall where they were shot?' he cried.

Wonderingly we all looked at the bullet holes, still clear and sharp.

'Which one killed Corporal Perkins?' demanded the boy. 'This one, that one?'

I shook my head as Rose put her hand in mine.

'There's no telling,' I said, 'it's all one now. This place, that place, the bullet or the sword. Men who died for a faith, God rest them all.'

But for a brief moment I saw only flaxen hair in the morning light blown across the churchyard wall.

'We have not forgotten,' I said and took my son's hand as we walked away.

Epilogue

REVERSAL OF SCRATCHING AND PLAQUE AT BURFORD CHURCH

The Restoration of the Stuart monarchy in the year 1660 was to me painful in the extreme. Not so much because I objected to the second King Charles in himself but because it brought back to me the tumultuous years of civil war and Interregnum.

Those were years of such anguish, torment and pain both personal and national that I thought never to have reminded myself of them. But, indeed, I need no reminder. The memories, the agony, the tumult crowd in… I had to purge my spirit by writing. And perhaps, in so doing, I may have come closer to an understanding of those events and an understanding of myself.

But I have written not for the world at large. Nor have I written as I did then, with the words tumbling out red hot for the secret presses. I have written soberly for my son, soberly and with consideration for him and his children and his children's children. I have omitted nothing. If I am to be judged, let it be in the light of my whole life, of all my actions.

God bless you who have read this. May He guide you with a greater certainty of right and wrong than was ever understood by

Anthony Sedley

Printed in Great Britain
by Amazon

81282549R00149